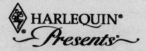
HARLEQUIN®
Presents

To all readers of Harlequin Presents

Thank you for your loyal
custom throughout 2006.

We look forward to bringing you the best
in intense, international and provocatively
passionate romance in 2007.

Happy holidays, and all good wishes
for the New Year!

Men who can't be tamed…or so they think!

If you love strong, commanding men,
you'll love this miniseries.

Meet the guy who breaks the rules to get
exactly what he wants, because he is…

HARD-EDGED & HANDSOME
He's the man who's impossible to resist…

RICH & RAKISH
He's got everything—and needs nobody…
Until he meets one woman….

He's RUTHLESS!
In his pursuit of passion; in his world
the winner takes all!

Brought to you by your favorite
Harlequin Presents® authors!

Coming in January:

At the Spaniard's Convenience
by Margaret Mayo
#2562

HARLEQUIN®
Presents

To all readers of Harlequin Presents

Thank you for your loyal
custom throughout 2006.

We look forward to bringing you the best
in intense, international and provocatively
passionate romance in 2007.

Happy holidays, and all good wishes
for the New Year!

RED HOT REVENGE

There are times in a man's life...

when only seduction will settle old scores!

Pick up our exciting series of revenge-filled
romances—they're recommended and red-hot!

Available only from Harlequin Presents®

Miranda Lee

PLEASURED IN THE BILLIONAIRE'S BED

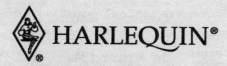

TORONTO • NEW YORK • LONDON
AMSTERDAM • PARIS • SYDNEY • HAMBURG
STOCKHOLM • ATHENS • TOKYO • MILAN • MADRID
PRAGUE • WARSAW • BUDAPEST • AUCKLAND

ISBN-13: 978-0-373-12588-3
ISBN-10:   0-373-12588-7

PLEASURED IN THE BILLIONAIRE'S BED

First North American Publication 2006.

Copyright © 2006 by Miranda Lee.

This edition published by arrangement with Harlequin Books S.A.

www.eHarlequin.com

Printed in U.S.A.

All about the author...
Miranda Lee

MIRANDA LEE was born in Port Macquarie, a popular seaside town on the mid-north coast of New South Wales, Australia. Her father was a country schoolteacher and brilliant sportsman. Her mother was a talented dressmaker.

After leaving her convent school, Miranda briefly studied the cello before moving to Sydney, where she embraced the emerging world of computers. Her career as a programmer ended after she married, had three daughters and bought a small acreage in a semirural community.

Miranda attempted greyhound training, as well as horse and goat breeding, but was left dissatisfied. She yearned to find a creative career from which she could earn money. When her sister suggested writing romances, it seemed like a good idea. She could do it at home, and it might even be fun!

It took a decade of trial and error before her first romance, *After the Affair,* was accepted and published. At that time, Miranda, her husband and her three daughters had moved back to the central coast, where they could enjoy the sun and the surf lifestyle once again.

Numerous successful stories followed, each embodying Miranda's trademark style: fast-paced and sexy rhythms; passionate, real-life characters; and enduring, memorable story lines. She has one credo when writing romances: Don't bore the reader! Millions of fans worldwide agree she never does.

CHAPTER ONE

LISA grimaced when the couple on the television screen started ripping each other's clothes off.

'As if people *really* act like that,' she muttered as she reached for the remote.

If there was one thing Lisa couldn't stand it was over-the-top love scenes in movies. As much as she appreciated she might not be a typical viewer, Lisa felt pretty sure sex was never the way it was portrayed in Hollywood.

She literally cringed when the man lifted the by now half-naked woman onto the kitchen counter and thrust into her. Or pretended to. The camera was on their faces. When the grunting and groaning started, Lisa pressed her finger firmly on the off button. She'd had enough of watching such ridiculous goings-on, thank you very much. Time to go upstairs and make sure Cory was asleep. It was after nine o'clock and tomorrow was a school day.

Lisa was halfway up the stairs when the phone rang.

Darn, she thought as she hurried on up the stairs and turned left, popping her head into Cory's bedroom on the way to her own bedroom.

Good, he was asleep.

Once in her bedroom, she closed the door behind her—so as not to risk waking her son—and picked up the cordless phone.

'Hello,' she said, fully expecting it to be her mother at this hour. All her girlfriends were married with children and were too busy each evening for gossipy chats.

'It's Gail, Lisa,' a woman's voice said down the line. 'Gail Robinson.'

Lisa decided she'd best sit down. When one of her employees rang her on her personal line on a week night, it usually meant there was some problem or other.

'Hi, Gail. What's up?'

'I've sprained my ankle,' Gail said dispiritedly. 'Slipped down that rotten steep driveway of ours. I've been sitting here with my foot in a bucket of iced water for ages but it's still up like a balloon. There's no way I can do Jack Cassidy's place tomorrow.'

Lisa frowned. Jack Cassidy was one of her newer clients. Sandra—her assistant-cum-bookkeeper—had signed him up whilst Lisa was away with Cory on a week's cruise of the South Pacific during the recent school holidays. A bachelor, Mr Cassidy owned a penthouse apartment in Terrigal which apparently had acres of tiled floors and took ages to clean. He also liked his sheets and towels changed and his weekly linen washed, dried and put away, not something her cleaners usually did. Their standard service lasted four hours and covered cleaning all floors, bathrooms and kitchens, not doing laundry or windows. Laundry could be very time-consuming and windows dangerous.

But he'd apparently talked Sandra into finding someone who would do the extra.

Gail took five hours to do everything, for which Clean-in-a-Day was paid one hundred and fifty dollars, with Gail's cut being one hundred and twenty. Their rates were very competitive.

'I'm really sorry to let you down at the last minute,' Gail said unhappily.

'That's all right. I'll get someone else.'

'On a Friday?'

Lisa knew why Gail sounded sceptical. Friday was the busiest day for housecleaning. Everyone wanted their homes to be clean for the weekend. Clean in a Day was fully booked on Fridays. Lisa had a couple of names she could ring if she was really desperate, but they were women who had not been through her rigorous training course and might not clean as thoroughly as she liked.

'Don't worry,' she said briskly. 'I'll do it myself. And Gail...'

'Yes?'

'Don't stress about the money. You'll still get paid.'

'Are you serious?'

'I'm well aware how tight things are for you at the moment.'

Gail's husband had been made redundant a few weeks earlier. She really needed her cleaning money.

'That's very good of you,' she choked out.

Lisa winced. Dear heaven, please don't let her start crying.

'Will you be up at the school tomorrow afternoon to pick up the kids?' she asked quickly.

'Yes.'

'I'll give you your money then.'

'Gosh, I don't know what to say.'

'Don't say a word. Especially not to the other girls. Can't have my sergeant-major reputation tarnished. They'll think I've become a soft touch and start taking advantage.'

Gail laughed. 'I can't see that happening. You have a very formidable air about you, you know.'

'So I'm told.'

'You always look so perfect as well. That's rather intimidating.'

'It's just the way I am,' she said defensively.

Lisa had heard such criticisms before. From girl-friends. From her mother. Even her husband. When he'd been alive…

Greg had complained incessantly about her compulsive need to have everything look right all the time. The house. The garden. Herself. The baby. Him.

'Why don't you lighten up a bit?' he'd thrown at her more than once. 'You're nothing like your mother. She's so easygoing. I thought daughters were supposed to be like their mothers!'

Lisa shuddered at the thought of being like her mother.

Despite Greg's nagging, she held on to the belief he hadn't *really* wanted her to be like her mother. He'd certainly liked inviting people back to their house, knowing she and it would always be neat and tidy.

'By the way, I don't have keys to Mr Cassidy's place,' Gail said, reefing Lisa's mind back to the problem at hand. 'He's always home on a Friday. I just press the button for the penthouse at the security entrance and he lets me in.'

Lisa's top lip curled. Pity. She hated having a client around when she cleaned.

'He's a writer of some sort,' Gail added. 'Works from home.'

'I see.'

'Don't worry. He won't bother you. He stays in his study most of the time. Only comes out to make coffee. Which reminds me. Don't attempt to clean his study. Or even to go in. He made that clear to me on my first day. His study is off limits.'

'That's fine by me. One less room to clean.'

'That's exactly what I thought.'

'Will I have a parking problem?' Lisa asked.

Terrigal was *the* place to live on the Central Coast. Only an hour and a half's drive north from Sydney, it had everything to attract tourists. The prettiest beach. Great shops and cafés. And a five-star hotel, right across from the water.

The only minus was demand for parking spaces.

'No worries,' Gail said. 'There are several guest bays at the back of the building. You have the address, don't you? It's on the main drag, halfway up the hill, just past the Crowne Plaza.'

'I'll find it. Well, I'd better get going, Gail. Have to have everything shipshape tonight if I'm to be out all day tomorrow.'

Which she would be. Terrigal Beach was a good fif-teen-minute drive from where she lived at Tumbi Umbi. If she dropped Cory off at school at nine, she'd be cleaning by nine-thirty, finished by two-thirty, then back to pick up Cory at three.

'See you at the school around three. Bye.'

Lisa hung up and hurried back downstairs, making a mental list of jobs-to-do as she went. Load dishwasher. Hang out washing. Wipe over tiles. Iron Cory's uniform. Get both their lunches ready. Decide what to wear.

Loading the dishwasher wasn't exactly rocket science and Lisa found her thoughts drifting to tomorrow.

Penthouses in Terrigal were not cheap. So its owner was probably rich.

A writer, Gail had said. A successful writer, obviously.

No, not necessarily. Jack Cassidy could be a wealthy playboy who'd inherited his money and dabbled in writing as a hobby.

When Lisa started wondering if he was good-looking, she pulled herself up quite sharply. What did she care if he was good-looking or not?

She had no intention of dating, or ever getting married again. She had no reason to. And she had every reason not to.

For once you let a man into your life, sooner or later he would want sex.

The unfortunate truth was Lisa didn't like sex. Never had. Never would. No use pretending.

She found sex yucky. And no pleasure at all. Not quite repulsive, but close to.

She'd suspected this about herself from the moment her mother had told her the facts of life at the age of ten, a suspicion which had grown over her teenage years, then was confirmed, at the age of nineteen, when she'd finally given in and slept with Greg. Though only after they'd got engaged. And only because she'd known she'd lose him if she didn't.

He'd thought she would warm to lovemaking in time. But she never had. Sex during her marriage had been given grudgingly, and increasingly less often with the passing of time, especially after Cory was born. It was not surprising that she hadn't fallen pregnant again.

Lisa had been shattered by her husband's tragic death when she was twenty-five and poor Greg only twenty-eight. She had loved him in her own way. But she never wanted to go there again. Never wanted to feel guilty about something she had no control over.

Lisa knew she could never force herself to like physical intimacy. So the only sensible solution was to remain single and celibate, even if it meant she sometimes felt lonely.

Lately, she'd been feeling very lonely. Which was odd. She was busier than ever with the business. And her son was always on the go. Her leisure hours were filled with taking him to his various school and sporting activities.

It was at night, after Cory had gone to bed, that she felt the loneliest. She missed having someone there to talk to. Or to sit with whilst she watched television.

Her one solace was reading. She loved books, especially thrillers. Loved the way they could take her away from her day-to-day, rather humdrum existence into a world of excitement and suspense. Her current favourites were a series of action novels written by an Australian author, Nick Freeman.

Lisa had never read anything like them. They were simply unputdownable. During the last few months, she'd devoured all five of them.

Unfortunately, she'd finished the last one a few nights back, and passed it on to her mother, as she had the others in the series.

By comparison, the new book by another author that she'd brought home from the library yesterday seemed tame. And boring. Which meant she wasn't looking forward to going to bed tonight, as she had when she knew she was going to be swept away into Hal Hunter's rather wicked but fascinating world.

Whenever Lisa didn't have a good book to read at night, sleep would often elude her. She suspected that tonight would be one such night.

'Cleaning that penthouse tomorrow will do you good, Lisa, my girl,' she told herself as she closed the dishwasher door. 'Make you really tired.'

The thought occurred to her that she should ring Jack Cassidy and let him know of the change in his cleaning arrangements. It could prove awkward, explaining things on his doorstep in the morning.

Lisa turned on the dishwasher and trudged back upstairs, turning right this time and making her way down to the fourth bedroom, which she'd converted into a study soon after starting up her business. It was not a large room, but large enough to house her computer.

It only took her a few seconds to bring up Jack

Cassidy's file and to print out his address and phone number.

Lisa picked up her fax-phone, punched in the number, than sank back into her office chair as she waited for her client to answer.

Several rings went by before a deep, gruff voice snapped, 'Yep?'

'Mr Cassidy?' she said in her best business voice. 'Mr Jack Cassidy?'

'Yeah, that's me. And who might you be?'

'My name is Lisa, Mr Cassidy. Lisa Chapman. I'm from—'

'Stop right there, sweetheart. Look, I know you're probably only doing your job but I've had a gutful of telemarketers ringing me at all hours of the day and night. This is my private and personal number and I keep it for private and personal calls. If I want something, I go out and buy it. From a shop. I don't even buy over the internet. I also never answer stupid bloody surveys. Do I make myself clear?'

Clear as crystal, Lisa thought with a mixture of empathy and frustration. She too hated people trying to sell things to her over the phone and had recently started being less than polite when telemarketers called her in the evenings.

But he could have had the decency to wait till he found out if she *was* one of those.

Lisa opened her mouth to clarify her identity when she heard the unmistakable click of the call being terminated.

Her head jerked back to stare down at her handset. He'd hung up on her! The hide of him!

After slamming her own phone back down, Lisa sat there for a full minute with her hands clenched over the arm-rests of the chair and her teeth gritted together. Never in all her life had anyone hung up on her. Never ever!

Don't take it personally, her brain argued.

But it was difficult not to. Men were supposed to be polite to women, no matter what. And he'd been rude. *Very* rude.

What to do? No point in trying his number again. He'd probably hang up on her before she got two words out. And if he did that, she'd blow a gasket.

She glared at his printed-out file. It showed no email number. Clearly, he was a privacy freak. Or he just didn't like computers. Or the internet. Maybe he wrote in longhand.

He did have a fax number, she noted. She could send him a fax, explaining the situation. But something inside Lisa rebelled against giving Jack Cassidy that courtesy.

No, she would just show up on his doorstep in the morning and have great pleasure watching him cringe with embarrassment, once she explained who she was.

CHAPTER TWO

LISA'S stomach tightened as she drove across Terrigal Bridge and turned left at the small roundabout.

Maybe it hadn't been such a good idea not to fax Jack Cassidy last night. Embarrassing the man no longer held such appeal this morning. *She* was the one who was going to end up being embarrassed.

Lisa scooped in a deep, lung-filling breath as she drove up the hill, then let it out slowly, relaxing her stomach muscles and reassuring herself that there was nothing for *her* to be embarrassed about. Or to feel nervous about. She was being silly. This was just another cleaning job. One she'd never have to repeat, thank goodness.

Feeling marginally better, Lisa glanced around as she drove down the hill which led to Terrigal Beach. She hadn't been out this way for ages. When she took Cory to the beach these days, they usually went to Wamberal, or Shelly's Beach. Terrigal's cove-like shape meant it rarely had a big surf, which was great for tourists and families, but not relished by nine-year-old thrill-seekers.

But my, it was beautiful, especially when the sun

was shining. Although it was still only springtime, the beach had a fair share of people in the water, and even more stretched out on the golden sand.

Lisa could see why wealthy Sydneysiders bought beach-houses here. And penthouse apartments. Especially ones whose balconies faced north, with an unimpeded view of the sparkling blue sea and the long stretch of coastline.

Jack Cassidy's place would have all that, Lisa realised by the time she turned into the driveway of the pale blue, cement-rendered apartment block. Despite the building only being three storeys high, its position was second to none.

Lisa's nervous tension had returned with a vengeance by the time she walked round to the front entrance and pressed the button marked 'Penthouse' on the security panel.

'Come on up, Gail,' Jack Cassidy's deep male voice growled through the intercom.

Lisa opened her mouth to explain once again who she was when the intercom clicked off and the front door began to buzz.

Giving vent to a groan of sheer frustration, Lisa pushed her way in, the door automatically closing and locking behind her.

She just stood there for a long moment, trying to calm her thudding heart. What was it about this man which rattled her so? She was normally very cool when it came to dealing with difficult clients and situations. Cool and composed.

Time for some coolness and composure right now,

Lisa, she lectured herself as she practised some more deep breathing, taking in her surroundings at the same time.

The foyer was cool and spacious, with a marble-tiled floor and lots of windows. Despite the amount of glass, you couldn't hear the traffic or the sea from inside, which meant the windows had to be double-glazed. A no-expense-spared building, Lisa conceded as she bypassed the lift at the back of the foyer to take the stairs, walking briskly up the grey-carpeted steps to the top floor.

No large foyer up there. Possibly the architect hadn't wanted to waste valuable floor space, although the landing was large enough to have a hall stand and wall mirror set beside the one and only door, perhaps put there for people to check their appearance before knocking.

Before she could do little more than give her face a cursory glance, the door was wrenched open by a very tall, very tanned, very fit-looking man in dark blue jeans and a chest-hugging white T-shirt.

Jack Cassidy, Lisa presumed, her neck craning a little as she looked up into his face.

He wasn't handsome. Not the way Greg had been handsome. But he *was* attractive, despite the three-day growth on his chin and the hard, almost cold grey eyes which swept over her from head to toe.

'You're not Gail,' were his first words, delivered with his now familiar lack of charm.

Lisa bristled inside, but maintained what she hoped was a professional expression.

'You're absolutely correct,' came her crisp reply. 'I'm Lisa Chapman from Clean-in-a-Day. Gail sprained her ankle yesterday and won't be able to do your place today. I did try to explain this to you last night on the phone, but you hung up on me.'

He didn't look embarrassed at all. He just shrugged. 'Sorry. You should have said who you were up front.'

If apologies had been an Olympic event, his would not have even qualified for a semi-final.

'You didn't exactly give me much opportunity,' she said with a tight little smile. 'But not to worry. I'm here now and I'll be doing your place today.'

'You have to be kidding me.'

Lisa gritted her teeth. 'Not at all.'

His eyes flicked over her again, this time with a coolly sceptical expression. 'You're going to clean in that get-up?'

'I don't see why not,' came Lisa's tart reply.

She had never subscribed to the theory that a cleaner had to look like a chimney sweep. Today she was wearing white stretch Capri pants, white trainers and a chocolate-brown singlet top which showed off her nicely toned arms and honey-coloured skin. Her platinum-blonde hair was up in a white scrunchie, the way she always wore it when cleaning. Her jewellery was a simple gold chain around her neck, a narrow gold watch on her wrist and small gold hoops in her ears. Her make-up was subtle and so was her perfume. In her roomy straw hold-all—currently slung over her shoulder—was a navy, chef-size apron and two pairs of cleaning gloves, along with her calorie-friendly packed lunch and a bottle of chilled mineral water.

'I assure you I will leave here with your place

spotless and without a mark on my clothes,' she informed him, a tad haughtily.

'You know what, sweetheart? I believe you.'

Lisa gritted her teeth. She was within a hair's breadth of telling him she was not his sweetheart, but the owner of Clean-in-a-Day, when he stepped back and waved her inside.

The uninterrupted sight of the spectacular living area compelled Lisa to forget her irritation, her love of all things beautiful drawing her forward till she was standing in the middle of the spacious room, surrounded by the sort of place she dreamt about owning one day. She almost sighed over the huge tinted windows, the amazing view, the acres of cream marble tiles and the wonderfully clean lines of the furniture. Nothing fussy. Everything classy and expensive. Cool leathers, in cream and a muted gold colour. The coffee- and side-tables were made of a pale wood. The rugs blended in. Nothing bright or gaudy.

Ever since she'd been a child, Lisa had hated bright colours, both in décor and clothes. She could not bear the recent fashion of putting loud, clashing colours together, oranges with pinks, and electric blues with lime greens. She literally shuddered whenever she saw red anywhere near purple.

'I do realise that there are a lot of tiles to clean,' he said abruptly from just behind her. 'But Gail never had a problem.'

Lisa swung round to face him, grateful that he hadn't thought she'd been envying him his house.

'They won't be any problem to me, either,' she said swiftly. 'I've been cleaning houses for years.'

'You continue to amaze me. You look like you've never had a chipped fingernail in your life.'

'Looks can be deceiving, Mr Cassidy.'

'For pity's sake, call me Jack. Now, a few instructions before I get back to work. Do you know about the extras I like done?'

'You wish your sheets and towels to be changed, washed, dried and put away.'

His eyebrows lifted, then fell, his expression betraying a slight disappointment that he hadn't caught her out in some way.

'You'll find everything you need in the laundry,' he told her. 'My bedroom is the last door on the left down that hallway,' he said, pointing to his right. 'My study is the first door. Did Gail warn you I don't like to be disturbed when I work?'

'She did mention it. She said you were a writer of some sort.'

Lisa almost asked him what kind of books he wrote, but pulled herself up in time. She'd always instructed her cleaners during their training never to become too familiar with male clients, especially ones who were in the house whilst they cleaned.

The corner of his mouth lifted in a wry fashion. 'Yeah. A writer of some sort just about describes me at the moment.'

The sound of a telephone ringing somewhere in the penthouse brought a scowl to his face. 'Damn! I should have switched on the answering machine. Still, I doubt it's telemarketers at this hour in the morning. I'd better answer the darned thing,' he grumbled before turning and marching off down the hallway to his right. 'You might not see me later,' he called back over his shoulder. 'I'm on a deadly deadline. Your money's on the kitchen counter. If I don't surface, just leave when you're finished.'

When he disappeared into his study and shut the door after him Lisa was flooded by a weird wave of disappointment.

The realisation that she'd actually been enjoying their conversation shocked her. What was there to like about it? Or about him?

Absolutely nothing, she decided emphatically as she whirled and went in search of the laundry.

CHAPTER THREE

JACK plonked himself down in front of his computer before snatching up the nearby phone.

'Jack Cassidy,' he answered, leaning back into his large and very comfy office chair.

'Jack, it's Helene.'

'I had a feeling it might be you,' he said drily. Helene hadn't become a top literary agent by letting her clients fall down on the job. This was her fourth call this week.

'Have you finished the book yet?'

'I'm on the last chapter.'

'Your publisher in London has been on to me again. He said if you don't deliver that manuscript by the end of this week, he might not be able to get it on the shelves for the British and North American summers. And you know what that means. Lower sales.'

'It'll be there, Helene. Tonight.'

'Is that a promise?'

'Have I ever let you down before?'

'No. But that's because I hound you to death. Which brings me to the other reason for this call. The annual literary-awards dinner is tomorrow night. You're the hot favourite for the Golden Gun award again, so you will show up, won't you?'

'Wild horses won't keep me away, Helene.'

Although he wasn't overly fond of award nights, Jack was actually looking forward to going out tomorrow night. It had been weeks since he'd socialised in any way, shape or form. Weeks, too, since he'd slept with a woman, a fact brought home to him this morning when he'd answered the door and found a drop-dead gorgeous blonde standing there, instead of plump, homely Gail.

Despite her hoity-toity, touch-me-not manner, Lisa Chapman had certainly reminded him that there was more to life than work.

Too bad she was married. Jack's observant eyes had noted the rings on her left hand within seconds of her introducing herself.

'Jack! Are you there?'

'Yeah, yeah, I'm here, Helene. Just wool-gathering.'

'Thinking about that last chapter, I hope.'

'All the time.'

Jack hated last chapters. He had a tendency to want to end his stories with a happily-ever-after scene. But that would be so wrong for a Hal Hunter book, especially at this stage in the series. Jack needed to come up with something seriously anti-heroish for his hero to do this time to finish up on. Couldn't have his readers start thinking Hal was some kind of saint, just because he went around making sure the baddies got their comeuppances.

Jack knew that it was Hal's political incorrectness which appealed to his fans. They enjoyed Hal doing what they would never dare do themselves. They thrilled to his ruthlessness, plus his uncompromising sense of justice and vengeance.

'I'd better get back to work, Helene.'

'Fine. But one last thing about tomorrow night. Do try to bring a girl who's read a book this time, will you?'

Jack laughed. The blonde he'd taken to the awards dinner last year had been none too bright, something he hadn't realised when he'd first met her on Bondi Beach and asked her to come with him. He'd been distracted at the time by how well she'd filled out her bikini.

By the end of the evening, any desire he'd originally felt for her had well and truly disappeared. He'd taken her straight home, much to her obvious disappointment.

'Look, I'll probably come alone.'

'I find that hard to believe. Jack Cassidy, without a gorgeous blonde on his arm?'

'I don't just take out blondes,' he protested.

'Yes, you do. The same way Hal does.'

Jack's eyebrows rose. He hadn't realised.

Still, there was no gorgeous blonde in his life at the moment, except for the very beautiful girl who was currently cleaning his penthouse.

If only she wasn't married...

Some people tagged Jack as a womaniser. But he wasn't. Married women were off limits in his view, no matter how attractive they were.

On the other hand, Hal *was* a womaniser. The so-called hero in Jack's books wouldn't have cared less if Lisa Chapman was married. Not one iota.

This last thought flashed a light on in Jack's head.

'Get off the phone, Helene. I've just had a brilliant idea for my last chapter.'

'Can I take any credit?'

'None whatsoever. I'll see you tomorrow night.'

Jack hung up and set to work with renewed gusto, plunging into the final chapter, smiling wickedly to himself as Hal blotted his hero status with the beautiful blonde housemaid who'd come to change the linen in his hotel room. She was married, of course. But she forgot about that once Hal went into seduction mode. The girl knew that he was just using her. But the fiery passion in his kisses proved irresistible. She felt powerless to say no, powerless to stop him.

Hal made love to her several times, making her do things she'd never done before. But she thrilled to her own unexpected wantonness.

The last page saw her dressing afterwards, then bending over the bed to kiss the tattoo on Hal's bare shoulder.

He didn't stir. He seemed to be asleep. He didn't want her any more and she knew it. She sighed as she left the room. Only then did Hal roll over and reach for a cigarette. He lit up and dragged in deeply. His eyes were blank and cold.

'Done!' Jack muttered as he punched in 'THE END', then copied everything onto two flash discs, putting one in his top-drawer and the other into the lead-lined safe he'd had built into the bottom drawer. Jack believed in solid security. He would read the last chapter through again later this afternoon before emailing the manuscript to London, but he felt sure he'd got it right.

Of course, there would be a hue and cry from his editor. She'd complain that his hero was getting too dark. But he'd weather the storm and have his way. And his readers would love it.

Jack chuckled when he thought of Hollywood's reaction. But they'd just have to like it or lump it as well. Helene had done a fabulous job, not only selling options for all the Hal Hunter books—including those not written yet—to a top movie studio for an absolute fortune, but also in forcing them to sign a rock-solid contract. They had to bring his books to the screen as he'd written them. No changes in titles, plot-lines, settings or characters. Definitely no changes to endings.

Jack wondered who they'd cast for the blonde in this last scene. Not anyone obvious or voluptuous, he hoped. Someone slender and classy-looking. Someone like Mrs Hoity-Toity out there.

Damn, but she'd stirred his hormones. A lot.

For a split-second, Jack toyed with the temptation of making her an indecent proposition. But he quickly got over it.

He was not Hal. He did not seduce married women.

Neither did he right the dreadful wrongs in this world.

That only happened in fiction. In the real world, the baddies didn't get their comeuppances. They lived on with their millions and their mistresses. They destroyed countries and slaughtered innocent people, but rarely faced punishment.

Jack grimaced. Not that bandwagon again, he

lectured himself. There was nothing you could do back then. Nothing you could *ever* do. None of it was your fault.

Jack's brain knew that. But his heart didn't always feel the same, that unexpectedly sensitive heart which had been stripped bare by his experiences in the army.

Despite not having worn a soldier's uniform for six years, the memories of all Jack had witnessed still haunted him. He would never forget. Or forgive.

But at least now, with the success of his books, he'd rediscovered some pleasure in living.

Which brought him right back to one pleasure he'd been doing without lately.

'What you need is to get laid,' he muttered to himself as he rose from his chair and left his study.

Lisa was bending over, about to take the towels out of the front-loading washing machine, when she sensed someone standing behind her.

Even before she straightened and spun around, she knew it was Jack Cassidy.

He was standing in the laundry doorway, watching her with those steely grey eyes of his.

'Can I help you?' she snapped, annoyed with the way her heart had started pounding.

'I didn't mean to startle you,' he returned. 'You can put my study on your cleaning list as well now. I've finished my book.'

'You want me to clean your study on top of everything else?' she asked, her voice still sharp.

'I'll pay you extra.'

'It's not a matter of money, Mr Cassidy, but time. I have to be gone from here by two-thirty to pick up my son from school.'

'I see. You can't get anyone else to pick him up?'

'No. I can't.'

'Could you come back tomorrow perhaps? My study hasn't been cleaned for a few weeks, and frankly, it's a mess.'

'I'm sorry, I can't do it tomorrow, either.' Lisa was beginning to regret not telling him she was the owner of Clean-in-a-Day, not just a contract cleaner. But it was too late now. He'd think she was weird for not mentioning it sooner.

'Why not?' he persisted. 'Will your husband object, is that it?'

'What? No. No, I don't have a husband,' she confessed.

'But you're wearing a wedding ring,' he said, confusion in his face and voice.

'I'm a widow.'

CHAPTER FOUR

Jack hoped he didn't look as gobsmacked by this news as he felt. Or as excited.

A widow no less. Now, that was a different ball game entirely.

'But you're so young,' he remarked whilst his brain started making plans which his body definitely approved of.

'I'm thirty,' she retorted.

'You don't look it.'

'I've always looked young for my age.'

'What happened to your husband?'

'He died in an accident, five years ago.'

'A car accident?'

'No. He fell off the roof of our house.'

'Good lord. That must have been dreadful for you.'

'It was,' she replied stiffly.

'Do you have any other children?'

'No. Just the one,' she told him. 'Cory. He's nine.'

Nine! She must have married very young. Either that, or she'd fallen pregnant *before* the wedding.

No. Jack didn't think that would have happened.

Mrs Lisa Chapman wasn't the sort of girl who had unplanned pregnancies.

'Is your son the problem, then?' he asked. 'Can't you get someone to look after him tomorrow morning?'

'No, I can't.'

Mmm. No live-in boyfriend, then.

He was tempted to suggest she bring the boy with her, but decided that was going a bit fast. Jack was smart enough to realise that was not the way to go with this particular lady. She was what he and his mates in the army had used to call an ice princess. Back then, they'd all steered well clear of ice princesses, none of them having the money or the time it took to melt them.

If he wanted to know his cleaner better—and his body kept screaming at him that he did—Jack would have to be super-patient. And super-subtle.

'OK,' he said with a nonchalant shrug. 'Tell me what else you've got left to do. It can't be the kitchen. I've just been through there and it positively gleamed at me.'

His compliment surprised Lisa. As did his change in manner. Where had the grumpy guy gone who'd answered the phone last night? *And* who'd let her in this morning?

Finishing his book had certainly changed his personality.

But Lisa could understand that. When she finished a job, she often experienced a rush of warmth and well-being.

Cleaning the kitchen in this penthouse had brought considerable satisfaction. But then, what a magnificent kitchen it was! Lisa had never seen anything like it before. The bench tops were made of cream marble.

The cupboards, a light warm wood. The appliances, stainless steel.

It had been such a pleasure to clean. As had the rest of the penthouse. But she hadn't finished yet.

'I have to iron these towels and put them away,' she said. 'And I haven't washed any of the tiles yet.'

'Aah yes, the dreaded tiles. What say you leave them and tackle my study instead?'

Lisa stared down at the tiles around her. They really needed doing. She would not feel right leaving them undone. Neither did she want to come back tomorrow morning. There was something about Jack Cassidy which still perturbed her. She wasn't sure what.

'If I hurry, I should be able to do everything,' she said. 'It's only ten past one.'

Jack could not believe it when she set to work at a speed which made his head spin. This girl was a cleaner to beat all cleaners. Focused, and very fast. By ten to two, all the tiled floors were shining and she bustled off in the direction of his study, vacuum cleaner and feather duster in hand.

There hadn't been a single opportunity to chat her up in any way. It was work, work and more work. His chances of asking her to come to the dinner with him tomorrow night were fast running out. On top of that, Jack wasn't sure she'd say yes, anyway. Not once today had she looked at him with any interest, which was highly unusual. Most women found him attractive.

Maybe she had a boyfriend. Or maybe he just wasn't her type.

This last thought rankled. But there wasn't much he could do about it. If she didn't fancy him, she didn't fancy him.

Shaking his head, Jack brewed himself some coffee and was about to take it out onto the terrace when she materialised in the kitchen doorway, a strange look on her face.

'Yes?' he said.

'Are you Nick Freeman?'

'That's the name I write under. Yes.'

'Oh, my!'

Jack wasn't sure if that was a sign she was a fan. Or not.

Either way, he'd finally snared her interest.

'You've read some of my books?' he asked.

'All of them.'

'And what did you think?'

'I loved them.'

Even better. Clearly, Nick Freeman was her type. Or maybe it was wicked old Hal which brought that excited sparkle into her lovely blue eyes.

'Now, that's music to a writer's ears. Come and have coffee with me and tell me more.'

'But I haven't finished your study yet. In fact, I've hardly started. When I saw your books on the shelves, I...I—'

'Forget the study,' he interrupted, pleased as punch with this development. 'I'd much rather have my ego stroked. How do you like your coffee?'

'What? Oh—er—black, with no sugar.'

'A true coffee-lover. Like me,' he added with a smile.

'Now, don't give me any more objections, Lisa. I'm the boss here.'

She didn't like taking orders, he could see. Or not finishing her job. But he insisted and she grudgingly complied, sitting opposite him at the table on the terrace, primly sipping her cup of coffee whilst he attempted to draw her out some more.

Jack was careful not to stray from the subject of books. He'd noted that the moment he'd smiled at her, a frosty wariness had crept into her face.

She was widely read, he soon realised. And very intelligent. Clearly, she was wasted as a cleaner.

When she started glancing at her wrist-watch, however, Jack decided he could not wait much longer before making his move. If he let her leave, she might never come back. Next Friday, it would be homely Gail showing up to clean his penthouse and that would be that.

'I have to go to the annual literary-awards dinner tomorrow night in Sydney,' he said. 'One of my books is a finalist in the Golden Gun award for best thriller of the year.'

She put down her cup. 'Which one?'

'The Kiss Of Death.'

'Oh, you'll win. That was a great book.'

'Thank you. You're very kind. Actually, I was wondering if you'd like to come with me.'

Jack had had various reactions from women to his asking them out. But not once had a female stared at him the way Lisa Chapman was currently staring at him. As if he'd asked her to climb Mount Everest. In her bare feet.

'You mean…as your date?' she choked out.

'Yes, of course.'

She blinked, then shook her head.

'I'm sorry. I don't date.'

Jack could not have been more stunned. Didn't *date*? What kind of crazy lifestyle was that for a beautiful young woman whose husband had been dead for five years?

'What do you mean, you don't date?' Jack shot back at her.

Her eyes flashed resentment at him for questioning her. 'I mean, I don't date,' she repeated firmly.

'Why on earth not?'

She stood up abruptly, her shoulders straightening, her expression turning haughty. 'I think that's my private business, don't you?'

Jack stood up also, his face just as uncompromising. 'You can't blame me for being curious. And for being disappointed. I was enjoying your company just now. I thought you were enjoying mine.'

She looked a little flummoxed by this last statement. 'Well, yes, I was,' she said, almost as though the concept surprised her.

'Then come to the dinner with me.'

She hesitated, but then shook her head again, quite vigorously. 'I'm sorry. I…I can't.'

Can't, she'd said. Not *won't*.

Can't suggested there was some other reason why she was saying no. Other than her ridiculous claim that she didn't date.

The penny suddenly dropped. Maybe she had no

one to mind her son. And not enough money to pay for a sitter. Cleaners who only worked during school hours couldn't earn all that much. Maybe she didn't have any suitable clothes, either. Despite her very smart appearance today, Jack knew evening wear cost a lot.

'I'll pay for a sitter,' he offered. 'And buy you a suitable dress, if you don't have one.'

Her mouth dropped open again, her eyes glittering this time with more anger than shock. 'I have more than enough money to do both,' she snapped. 'For your information, Mr Cassidy, I am not an employee of Clean-in-a-Day. I own the company!'

For the second time that day, Jack was totally gob-smacked. Then pretty angry himself. 'Well, why didn't you say so? Why pretend you were a lowly cleaner?'

'*Lowly*? What's lowly about being a cleaner? It's honest work, with honest pay.'

'Yes, you're right. I shouldn't have said that.'

'No, you shouldn't. And you shouldn't have tried to buy me just now. Maybe that's what men do in your world, but they don't in mine.'

'I wasn't trying to buy you.'

'Yes, you were,' she said, crossing her arms and giving him a killer look. 'Don't try to weasel your way out of it.'

Jack could feel his level of frustration rising as it hadn't risen in years. 'Why don't you get off your high horse for a moment and stop overreacting! I wasn't trying to buy you. I was trying to overcome any obstacles which I thought might be in your path. Because I can't believe that a beautiful young woman like yourself would *choose* not to date. I presumed it had to be because of some other reason.'

'Then you'd be wrong. I *did* choose not to date after my husband died.'

'But that doesn't make sense, Lisa. Most young widows marry again. How do you expect to meet anyone if you lock yourself in your house and never go out?'

'I don't lock myself in my house. And I have no intention of *ever* getting married again.'

Jack noted the emphasis on the *ever*, plus the emotional timbre of her voice. Clearly, this was a subject which touched a nerve.

An old friend of Jack's—an army widow—had once told him that there were two reasons women decided not to marry again. They either had been so happy and so in love with their husbands they believed no other man would ever compare. Or they had been so miserable, they didn't want to risk putting their lives into the hands of a rotter a second time.

Jack didn't know enough about Lisa yet to decide which was her reason.

'Fair enough,' he said. 'I don't want to get married, either, even *once*. But don't you get bored? And lonely?'

A frustrated-sounding sigh escaped her lips as she uncrossed her arms. 'Boredom and loneliness are not the worst things in this world.'

'They come pretty high on my list.' Jack had a very low boredom threshold. He liked to keep active when he wasn't writing. During the winter he skied and went snow-boarding. In the summer he surfed and water-skied. When he was forced indoors by the weather, he worked out. Obsessively.

'Give me one good reason why you don't date and we'll leave it at that.'

She pursed her lips at him, her chin lifting. 'One good reason,' she repeated tartly. 'No trouble. When a single mother goes out with a man these days, he expects more than a goodnight kiss at the door. He wants to come inside and stay the night. No way would I have my son wake up in the morning to some strange man at the breakfast table. If I'm a little lonely sometimes, then that's the price I have to pay for giving my boy the example of good moral standards.'

Jack was impressed, but not entirely convinced. He feared she protested too much. There was something else here, something she wasn't admitting to. But he could see she wasn't about to confide in him at this early stage. If he could somehow persuade her to come out with him tomorrow night, he might eventually uncover some of the mystery behind this intriguing ice princess.

'I promise I won't expect more than a goodnight kiss at the door,' he said.

Now she looked seriously rattled. And tempted. Oh, yes, she was tempted. He could see it in her eyes.

'I'm sorry,' she said again after a more lengthy hesitation. 'My answer's still no. Now I really must go. I'm running late.'

Jack didn't try to stop her from leaving. He even reminded her about the money on the counter, which she almost forgot. But he took comfort from her obvious fluster. She'd definitely wanted to say yes to him. Or, if he was strictly honest with himself, she'd wanted to say yes to Nick Freeman.

It didn't really matter. They were one and the same, as she would find out, when she went to the dinner with him tomorrow night.

Jack had her phone number somewhere. At least, he had the phone number for Clean-in-a-Day. He would ring later this evening, after her boy had gone to bed. By then, Jack would have all his arguments ready to get her to change her mind.

And he would *not* take no for an answer!

CHAPTER FIVE

'MUM!' Cory exclaimed from the passenger seat. 'Where are you going?'

'What?'

'You drove straight past our street.'

Lisa sighed. It didn't surprise her. Since she'd left Jack Cassidy's place, it had been a struggle to keep her mind on what she was doing. She'd only just remembered to give Gail her money at the school.

Thank heavens Gail hadn't had time to chat. No way did Lisa want to talk about her day. She still hadn't come to terms with Jack Cassidy turning out to be Nick Freeman. *Or* with his asking her out to that awards dinner tomorrow night. *Or* her actually being tempted to say yes.

As Lisa negotiated the roundabout which would bring her back the way she'd come, she reiterated to herself that she'd done the right thing, saying no to his invitation.

She wasn't a complete fool. She could read between the lines. Jack Cassidy—alias Nick Freeman—was a ladies' man. Just like his character, Hal Hunter. Jack's penthouse had 'playboy pad' written all over it, from the indoor pool and spa to the private gym, the home theatre and the simply huge master bedroom, which had every seductive mod con built in. A huge plasma screen dominated the wall opposite the bed. There were dimmer switches on the lights. And a corner spa in the *en suite* bathroom definitely built for two. Or even three.

Aside from that, she'd noted his off-the-cuff remark that he didn't want to ever get married, even once. Yet he had to be in his mid-to-late thirties, past the age most men thought about settling down and having a family.

Clearly, his lifestyle of choice was that of swinging bachelor.

Mr Playboy would definitely not settle for a platonic peck at the door. He'd just been saying that to get her to go out with him. No doubt he thought she was an easy target, once he'd found out she was a widow.

Jack wasn't the first man to ask her out. But he was the first she'd been tempted to say yes to.

Why *was* that? Lisa asked herself as she drove slowly down her street.

His being her favourite author had to be the main factor. But she suspected it was also because a glamorous night out in Sydney was an exciting prospect for a suburban single mother who hadn't been anywhere glamorous in years. Up here on the coast, everything was very casual. You never got seriously dressed up for anything. Not even at Christmas.

Lisa loved getting dressed up. Or she had, when Greg had been alive.

Her wanting to say yes to Jack Cassidy's invitation had nothing to do with her finding him physically attractive, she told herself firmly. She liked slim, elegant-looking men with nice manners and soft blue eyes, not big, macho devils with faces carved out of granite and the coldest grey eyes she'd ever seen.

Lisa supposed Jack's surprise at her declaration that she didn't date was understandable. But she thought she'd handled the situation quite well. Of course, she hadn't been able to tell him the *real* reason she didn't date. That would have been embarrassing in the extreme.

Still, the reason she'd given was also true. She hated the way some single mothers went from man to man, most of whom didn't give a damn about their children. Yet they let these men into their children's lives; let the poor little mites get attached.

How many single mothers and divorcees actually found a decent fellow to marry? Not many. Once the man got bored with the sex, he moved on. She'd seen it happen amongst her women friends too many times to count, leaving behind broken hearts and sad, mixed-up children.

'Yes, I definitely did the right thing,' she muttered under her breath.

Her house came into view, a two-storeyed blond brick building which Lisa was very proud of, but which she'd struggled to keep after Greg died. His insurance payout had not covered the mortgage. But she'd been determined not to lose her home. And she hadn't, working very hard to make herself and her son financially secure. Even if she'd *wanted* to date, she hadn't had the time back then.

Lisa turned into her driveway, Cory jumping out of the car before she'd switched off the engine, bolting along the front path and dropping his school bag on the porch.

'Can I go and play up at Finn's place?' he called out as she climbed out of the car.

'Not until you've changed out of your uniform,' she told him sternly once she joined him on the porch. 'And done your homework.'

'But it's the weekend,' he protested. 'I can do my homework tomorrow.'

'No, you can't. You're going to your grandma's tomorrow while I go shopping. We both know there won't be any homework done there, don't we?' she added drily as she pulled the house keys from her bag.

'I'm glad I'm going to Grandma's,' Cory said, a belligerent look on his face. 'She lets me have fun. Not like you.'

'Don't you dare speak to me in that tone, young man,' Lisa snapped, jamming the key into the deadlock and thinking how thankless a job being a mother was. 'Now, get yourself inside and do as you're told.'

Five hours later, she was still brooding over Cory's cheekiness. And simmering with jealousy over his affection for his grandmother.

He didn't seem to care that his grandmother was the messiest woman on the planet. Always had been. Not only was Jill Chapman allergic to cleaning, but she couldn't cook to save her soul either. Lisa had grown up eating baked beans on toast for dinner most nights. Her mother's only talent was as a potter, and even then she didn't make much money at her craft.

'Mum,' Cory said in a wheedling tone, 'can I stay up and watch a movie with you tonight?'

Lisa glanced up from where she was stacking the dishwasher. Cory was a few feet away in the family room, watching TV.

'I don't think so, Cory. You've had a long week at school and I don't want you all tired and grumpy tomorrow. Off to bed now. It's eight-thirty.'

'Oh, Mum, *please*.'

'Not this time,' she said firmly.

'You never let me do anything,' he grumbled.

'You can stay up extra late tomorrow night. We'll go to the video shop after I finish my shopping and get you whatever movie you like. Provided it's not too violent.'

His blue eyes lit up. 'You promise?'

'I promise.'

'Cool!'

Lisa smiled at her son's obvious delight. And his obeying her orders to go to bed without any further fuss. When she went upstairs five minutes later, his handsome little face was still beaming with happiness.

'Goodnight and God bless,' she murmured as she ruffled his soft blond hair, then bent to kiss him. 'Love you.'

'Love you, too, Mum,' he said, making her heart squeeze tight.

Lisa supposed there were some rewards in being a mother. But it was hard, not having a partner to help with the parenting.

Not that Greg had been a firm father. He'd been way too soft with Cory. Way too soft with her as well. He'd let her run the show. And whilst Lisa liked being the boss of the household, there had been times when she'd wished Greg had taken the reins. In hindsight, he'd been a nice, but weak man. He should not have put up with her denying him sex…

When those old feelings of guilt threatened, Lisa pulled herself up sharply. The past was the past. No point in becoming maudlin over it.

As she always did when she started worrying about things, Lisa worked, mopping the kitchen floor and hanging out the washing which she'd put in the machine earlier. After that she went upstairs to the third bedroom, where she kept her iron and ironing board.

A lot of women hated ironing. But Lisa found it quite therapeutic. She ironed everything, enjoying seeing the neat piles of freshly pressed things set out on the spare bed. She was tackling Cory's school shirts when the phone rang in her office, just across the hall. Knowing that the answering machine would pick up, she kept on ironing, keeping one ear open to see who it was. The office door was ajar and she could hear quite clearly. Her recorded voice came on first, asking the caller to leave a message after the beep.

When she heard Jack's deep male voice come on to the line, she almost dropped the iron.

'Jack Cassidy here, Lisa. Unfortunately, it seems I only have your business number. Hopefully, you're home and check your messages on a regular basis. If so, please call me back some time tonight. You have my number. If I don't hear from you by morning, I'll have to ring Gail and find out your home or mobile number.

I'm sure she'll have it. If you don't want me to do this—and I suspect you might not—then ring me. ASAP.'

After Jack had hung up, Lisa remained standing right where she was for several seconds, still gripping the iron mid-air. Her head had gone into a total whirl with his message, her heart racing like mad.

Eventually, she lowered the iron back onto its cradle, then sat down on the side of the bed whilst she assembled her scattered thoughts.

Somehow, she didn't think Jack wanted her to call him to organise another cleaner to do his study. If he had, he would have simply said so.

He was going to ask her out again. She was sure of it!

Lisa could not understand why. A man like him could have his pick of women. Why pursue her?

'Because you said no to him,' she muttered out loud.

Lisa could think of no other reason.

Under any other circumstances, she would have ignored his call. Lisa didn't like bully boys. But his threat to ring Gail in the morning was a worry. He was right. She wouldn't like that. Gail would jump to all the wrong conclusions and start gossiping about her and Jack.

She had no alternative but to ring the infernal man. But she intended to put him in his place. And tell him in no uncertain terms that she didn't appreciate being harassed, or threatened.

The thought of having a confrontation with him made her stomach churn. But it had to be done. And the sooner the better.

Steeling herself, Lisa stood up and marched across the hallway into her office. The piece of paper with Jack's number on it was still in the top drawer of her desk, Lisa's hand trembling slightly as she snatched up the phone.

He answered on the second ring, suggesting that he had been waiting for her call.

'I'm so glad you rang,' he said straight away in such a pleased voice that she felt some of her resentment drain away.

But her voice was still sharp.

'What is it that you want, Jack?'

You, Jack was tempted to reply. But didn't.

'I wanted to give you the chance to change your mind about tomorrow night,' came his diplomatic but still truthful reply.

He heard her sigh down the line. Unfortunately, it didn't sound like a sigh of pleasure. Or surrender. 'I won't change my mind, Jack.'

'Wait till you hear what I have to say.'

'Very well.'

'How long has it been since you've been taken out to dinner?'

Another exasperated sigh. 'I told you. I don't date.'

'How long, Lisa?'

'Over five years, I guess.'

'And how long since you've had a night out in Sydney?'

'About the same.'

Just as he had thought. She had to be one of the

loneliest girls in the world. And ripe and ready for some male attention.

'What if we don't call tomorrow night a date? Would that help? What if you think of it as a favour to a business client?'

'A favour?'

'A big favour. You've no idea what it's like going to these dos alone, Lisa. Which is what I'll have to do if you don't come with me.'

'Why would you have to go alone? There must be scads of women of your acquaintance who'd be only too happy to go with you.'

'Believe it or not, I'm not that social a guy. Or I haven't been, since buying this place a couple months back. I've had my nose to the grindstone for weeks, finishing that damned book. Hardly been outside the door, except for the occasional surf, or shop. Trust me when I say there's no one I could ask.'

'I find it hard to believe you don't have a little black book with loads of phone numbers in it.'

He did, actually. But he didn't want to ring any of them. All of the women in that book paled in comparison to the very lovely, very intriguing and very challenging Mrs Chapman.

'I think you're mixing me up with Hal,' Jack said. 'He's the one with the little black book.'

'Oh.'

'People do that a lot. Confuse me with Hal. Which is another reason why I want you to come with me tomorrow night. I get besieged by female fans at these awards dinners. He's a very popular guy, old Hal. Now, if I have a beautiful blonde on my arm, I just might survive the night in one piece. They'll take one look at you and know they don't have a hope in Hades of getting my personal attention.'

'I don't know, Jack…'

A rush of adrenalin charged through his blood. She was wavering.

'I promise I'll be a perfect gentleman all evening. You won't have to fight me off at the door.'

No answer.

'Think of the five-star food,' he went on seductively. 'And the five-star wine. Not to mention the five-star surroundings. This restaurant is top drawer, and right on the harbour, overlooking the bridge and the opera house.'

Her sigh this time sounded much closer to a sigh of surrender.

'You do know how to tempt a girl…'

'You'd be crazy not to come. I'll pick you up and deliver you home to your door. Minus the grope-fest.'

She actually laughed.

'It'll be a truly fun evening. How long is it, Lisa, since you've had fun?'

'Too long, my mother would say.'

'Your mother sounds like a wise woman. You should listen to her.'

'My mother wants me to get married again,' Lisa said drily.

'Mothers are like that.'

'Does your mother get on your back to get married, Jack?'

'My mother's dead,' came his rather curt reply.

'Oh. I'm sorry. I didn't think. I mean...you're not that old.'

'Both my parents were killed in a car accident when I was fifteen.'

'Oh, how tragic.'

'It was. The truck driver who killed them was unlicenced, driving an unsafe, unregistered vehicle. He got a miserable twelve months for murder.'

'Jack, that's appalling! You wonder what these judges are thinking of, giving light sentences like that.'

'Yeah, but it doesn't really hit home till it happens to you. Injustice is just a word till you experience it for yourself.'

'I suppose so,' Lisa murmured, thinking how dreadful to lose both one's parents like that. Her parents had been divorced, but it had been an amicable enough parting. Her perfectionist father hadn't been able to stand her mother's sloppy ways, and had bolted as soon as he found someone more to his liking.

He'd never come back.

Lisa might have resented his defection more if she'd been able to remember him. Or if she hadn't understood full well why he'd left. She'd left home, too, as soon as she could.

'I think we're getting too serious here,' Jack said. 'Back to tomorrow night. I presume you don't want to tell your mother you're going out with me.'

'If she found out I was going out anywhere with any man, she'd nag me to death. If she finds out I'm going to a fancy awards dinner with the famous Nick Freeman, I'd never hear the end of it.'

'She's a fan of Nick Freeman's?'

'Unfortunately. I introduced you to her a couple of months back.'

'Then don't tell her. It's not as though this dinner is going to be on TV, or anything like that. The only media coverage it'll get is in the *Australian Writers Monthly*. And who reads that, except the literati? I certainly don't.'

'You're very persuasive.'

'Is that a yes?'

'Yes. But…'

'No buts, Lisa. You're coming and that's that.'

'I was just going to say that I'll have to tell my mother I'm going somewhere with someone. She's the one who'll be minding Cory. I won't leave him with anyone else.'

'You're a woman. You'll think of something.'

'I don't have your imagination.'

Jack didn't think he had that great an imagination. Lots of things which happened in his books were things which had really happened. But he wasn't about to tell her that.

'Always stick as close to the truth as possible when you're being sneaky,' Jack suggested, thinking to himself that he had been doing just that. 'Why not say that a girlfriend of yours has been given two free tickets to the awards dinner and wants you to go with her? That way you can talk freely about your night out and not have to make anything up.'

'That's brilliant, Jack!'

'I *am* brilliant.'

'And so modest.'

'That, too.'

'But are you a man of your word?'

'Do you doubt it?'

'Hal's not always a man of his word.'

'I'm not Hal.'

'I'm not so sure. Your books are told in the first person.'

'That's just a tool to create immediate empathy with the reader. And a more intense emotional involvement with Hal's character.'

'You succeeded very well.'

'Thanks. Now, let's get off Hal for a moment. At the risk of offending you again, are you set, clothes-wise, for tomorrow night? It's black tie.'

'Do I have to wear a long evening dress?'

'Not necessarily. A cocktail or party dress will do fine.'

'I'll buy something tomorrow. I was going Christmas shopping, anyway.'

'Christmas shopping! But it's only October.'

'I don't like to leave present-shopping till the last minute,' came her prim reply. 'The pre-summer sales are on at Tuggerah tomorrow.'

'Where the hell is Tuggerah?'

'You don't know the coast too well, do you?'

'I know the Erina shopping centre. Why don't you go there? I could meet you and we could have coffee. Or lunch?'

'I don't think so, Jack. Don't forget, I'm only going with you tomorrow night as a favour. It is not a real date. It's a one-off. There won't be any encores. Or prequels. Take it or leave it, Jack.'

'I'll take it,' he said, and smiled to himself.

You can pretend to yourself all you like, sweetheart. But tomorrow night is not going to be any one-off. You like me. I can tell. Tomorrow night is just the beginning.

'I'll pick you up at six,' he added. 'That will give us plenty of time to get down to Sydney. Now, where do you live? Give me your address and some directions so that I don't get lost. And your mobile number, in case I need to contact you tomorrow and you're not home.'

'Why would you need to contact me?'

'The world's an unpredictable place, Lisa. I like to be prepared.'

'That's what Hal always says.'

'Does he? Well, I suppose I do have some things in common with my main man.'

Like his womanising ways, Lisa thought, suddenly concerned over her decision to go out with Jack.

What on earth had she been thinking when she let him change her mind?

She'd rung him up to put him in his place and ended up agreeing to be his pretend girlfriend for the night, letting him persuade her with the promise of adult company, great food and the fantasy of actually having some fun.

But what fun would it be if she was on tenterhooks all night, worried about fighting him off at the front door?

'You're not having second thoughts, are you?'

Lisa rolled her eyes. What was he, a mind-reader?

'Not at all,' she replied crisply. If he did try something when he brought her home, she'd be ready for him. He wouldn't get so much as a *toe* in her front door.

'How about your address and phone number, then? I have pen and paper at the ready.'

She gave him both, plus good directions. It was perfectly clear, however, that he hadn't been far afield from Terrigal, since he'd never heard of Tumbi Umbi Road.

'There's a Central Coast map in the local phone directory,' she said. 'Study it up.'

'I'll do that. And thanks, Lisa. I really appreciate your coming with me. You're a good sport.'

A good sport. Was that what playboys called foolish females these days?

'Bye for now,' he said breezily. 'See you tomorrow night.'

Tomorrow night...

Just the thought made her feel sick.

Oh, Lisa, Lisa, what have you done?

CHAPTER SIX

LISA'S chest tightened as it always did when she pulled into the driveway of her mother's place. Not so much these days because the ramshackle farmhouse would be a mess. But because her mother always seemed to say something to get her hackles up.

Lisa could hear implied criticism in even the most innocent of her mother's comments. As soon as she pulled up on the weed-filled patch of lawn which masqueraded as a front garden, Cory was out of the car like a shot, running up onto the veranda and giving his emerging grandma a big hug before dashing off to play on the tyre which swung from a nearby tree.

'Thanks for looking after Cory for me, Mum,' Lisa called out through the driver's window, trying not to really look at her mother. But it was impossible. Her hair was as red as the red in the multicoloured kaftan she was wearing. 'Not sure what time I'll be back. Probably not till after lunch.'

Lisa had decided on the way here not to tell her mother about going out tonight till she returned from shopping. She'd say she'd run into this mythical girlfriend at Tuggerah and been asked out when another girlfriend couldn't go with her.

'What's the hurry?' Jill Chapman called back as she walked down the rickety front steps. 'Can't you come in for a cup of coffee?'

'I'll do that when I come back. I don't want to be late. You know what the parking's like when the sales are on.'

'You look very nice today,' her mother said, drawing closer to the driver's window. 'There again, you always look nice. I wouldn't have thought you needed any new clothes.'

Lisa struggled to find a smile. 'Actually, I'm looking for Christmas presents today. But I think it's always good to buy a few new things at the start of each season,' she said through clenched teeth. 'Otherwise, your wardrobe ends up getting very dated.'

'Like mine, you mean,' her mother said with a hearty laugh.

'I didn't say that.'

'You didn't have to. I know I look like an escapee from the sixties most of the time. But that's what I am.'

Who would have guessed? Lisa thought wearily.

'I have to go, Mum,' she said. 'Keep an eye on Cory, would you? Don't let him wander off.' Her mother lived on a small acreage in the Yarramalong Valley, where there was a lot of bush. And snakes.

'He'll be fine.'

Lisa sighed under her breath as she waved goodbye and drove off. That was what her mother always said. And what she thought. Everything and everyone was always fine. Except her daughter, of course. Her daughter was a fussy, frigid fool who had no idea how to relax, or really enjoy herself.

Maybe she was right, Lisa conceded unexpectedly for the first time in her life. Here she was, going out to a slap-up dinner in Sydney tonight with her favourite author and was she happy? No! She was already worrying herself sick over how to act and what might or might not happen when Jack brought her home.

At least her mother was always happy. She'd been happy even after her husband left her.

I should be happy, Lisa lectured herself as she drove towards Tuggerah. I have a lovely home. A wonderful son. A flourishing business. And a good, if irritating, mother.

I also shouldn't be worrying about tonight. I am an adult woman, in control over what happens to me and what does not. If Jack makes a pass, I can handle it. There's no reason why I can't relax and enjoy myself.

The trouble was she always had difficulty relaxing. She seemed condemned to feel slightly uptight about everything, as if nothing was ever quite right, or good enough, or clean enough.

Lisa pulled a face. She was sick of this. Sick of herself.

Thank goodness it wasn't far from her mother's house to the shopping centre, the sight of Tuggerah ahead soothing her anxiety somewhat. Clothes shopping was one thing she *did* truly enjoy. She had a good sense of fashion and knew what suited her. When she'd attended the company Christmas parties with Greg he'd always been very proud of her.

Hopefully, Jack would feel just as proud when he came to pick her up tonight.

* * *

'You don't mind, Mum?' Lisa said, glancing up from where she was sitting at her mother's messy kitchen table, sipping coffee. The clock on the wall showed ten to one. Finding that special dress had taken Lisa longer than she'd anticipated.

'Mind? Why should I mind? I love having Cory over.'

'Where is he, by the way?'

'Down at the creek, looking for tadpoles.'

'He's OK by himself down there?'

'He can swim, can't he? Of course he's all right. You fuss over him too much, Lisa. Boys needs some space. And some freedom.'

'Maybe. But it's a dangerous world out there, Mum.'

'The world is whatever you believe it to be. I believe it to be good. And I believe people to be good. Until it's proven otherwise.'

Lisa sighed. Her mother was naïve, in her opinion. And out of touch. At the same time, she could see that Cory grew whenever he spent time with her. Not physically. But in maturity and experience. Her mother did allow him to do things she never would.

'It's good that you're going out,' her mother went on. 'Even if it is just with a girlfriend. So you're off to Sydney, are you? To a posh dinner in a posh restaurant. That's great. But watch yourself.'

Lisa blinked. 'What do you mean?'

'Sydney on a Saturday night can be a wild place. Don't go walking around the streets by yourself.'

'We're going to a restaurant, Mum. It's a literary-awards dinner with speeches and things. We won't be walking around the streets.'

'What are you going to wear?'

Lisa had decided not to show her mother the dress she'd bought. She wasn't in the mood for being criticised.

'I have plenty of party dresses in my wardrobe.'

'You know, you might see our favourite author there.'

'And who would that be?' Lisa said, trying to keep a straight face.

'Nick Freeman, of course. His books always win awards. It says so on the inside flaps. You'll have to tell me what he looks like. There's never a picture on the back cover. And not much of a biography. I think he writes under an assumed name.'

'He might be a woman,' came Lisa's oddly mischievous comment.

'Oh, no,' her mother said with a rather knowing smile. 'The creator of Hal is no woman. My guess is he's ex-military. He knows much too much about weapons not to have personal experience.'

'Maybe he just does a lot of research,' Lisa said, whilst thinking to herself that her mother was probably right.

'No. It's all too real. I sure hope he's going to write some more Hal Hunter books. I'm addicted to them already. Yet strangely enough, I think I like the first one the best. *The Scales of Justice*. That's where you really get to know Hal. You understand why he is the way he is after the way his parents get killed.'

Lisa frowned, only then making the connection

between Jack's parents being tragically killed and the way Hal's parents were killed. Not in a car accident. In a terrorist bombing.

Was that why Jack had become a loner, like Hal? Why he didn't want to marry and have a family of his own?

The answers to those questions possibly lay in that first book.

'You know, Mum, I think I'd like to read that one again. You haven't lent it to any of your friends, have you?'

'Nope. It's in my bedroom, under the bed. I'll go get it for you.'

Her mother had just left when the back screen door was yanked open and Cory charged into the kitchen, holding an old coffee jar full of muddy water.

The nicely washed and ironed clothes which she'd put on him that morning were also muddy. So was his face. It always pained Lisa to see her good-looking boy looking like a ruffian. But she held her tongue for once.

'Hi there, Mum! Where's Grandma?'

'Right here, sweetie,' Lisa's mother replied as she bustled back into the kitchen, handing Lisa the book before going straight over to Cory. 'Show me what you've got. Heavens! You've done well. We'll put them in the pond later. Hopefully, some of them might turn into frogs. By the way, you're staying the night,' she continued before Lisa could tell Cory herself. 'Your mum's going out to some fancy dinner in Sydney tonight.'

'Wow! Cool.'

Lisa wasn't sure if he meant it was cool she was going to Sydney, or cool that he was staying the night.

'Don't let him stay up too late,' she said.

Grandmother and grandson exchanged a conspiratorial glance. They were as thick as thieves, those two.

'It's Saturday night,' her mother said. 'Cory doesn't have to go to school tomorrow. He can sleep in in the morning. You're not going to be here to pick him up till lunch-time, I'll bet. It'll be *you* having the late night.'

Lisa didn't plan on being *that* late. But she didn't want to argue the point, for fear of making a slip-up with her story.

'Oh, all right,' she agreed. 'But not *too* late,' Lisa added as she picked up Jack's book and got to her feet. 'Don't go taking advantage of your grandmother, young man. And don't eat too much ice cream. You know what it does to your stomach.' Cory was lactose intolerant.

Cory's blue eyes went blank, exactly like his father's had when she used to nag him over something.

'Go give your mother a hug,' his grandmother said, giving Cory a nudge in the ribs.

'Be a good boy,' Lisa whispered as she held him to her for a little longer than she usually did.

His weary-sounding sigh made her feel guilty.

'Love you,' she added.

'Love you too, Mum,' Cory returned. But there wasn't a great deal of warmth in his words.

Suddenly, Lisa wanted to cry. And to keep holding him. Close.

But she knew he would hate that.

'See you tomorrow,' she choked out, struggling to keep back the tears as she let him go and hurried towards the door.

Her mother followed her out whilst Cory dashed off towards the pond with his jar of tadpoles.

'You all right, love?' her mother said.

Lisa tossed Jack's book onto the passenger seat as she climbed in behind the wheel. 'Yes, of course. Why shouldn't I be?'

'You seem a little more uptight than usual.'

'I'm not uptight at all,' Lisa suddenly snapped before banging the door shut and glaring at her mother through the open window. 'Why do you always criticise me, Mum? I've been a good daughter, haven't I? And I'm a good mother to Cory. I support myself and always try to do the right thing. So get off my back, will you?'

Regret at her sharp words consumed Lisa when her mother reeled back on her heels, shock in her eyes.

'I...I didn't realise,' her mother said, obviously shaken by Lisa having a go at her. 'I only ever want the best for you, love. But I can see I might have been a bit critical on occasions. Sorry. I'll try to keep my big mouth shut in future.'

Lisa was torn between feeling vindicated at having stood up for herself, and guilty over hurting her mother's feelings.

'I'm sorry, too, Mum,' she said. 'I know I'm touchy. I...I haven't been sleeping very well lately.'

'Then it will do you good to get out,' her mother said, all smiles again. Nothing ever got Jill Chapman down for long. 'Who knows? You might meet a man.'

'Mum...' Lisa warned.

'What's wrong with a mother wanting her beautiful daughter to meet a man?'

'You know I don't want to get married again.'

'So? I don't, either. But that's never stopped me having a boyfriend.'

'Or two,' Lisa muttered under her breath as she started the engine. 'Bye, Mum,' she said as she let go of the handbrake and moved off. 'See you in the morning.'

'No need to rush,' her mother shouted after her. 'Sleep in, if you want to.'

Lisa found herself shaking her head as she drove off. In a weird way, she wished she'd told her mother the total truth about tonight. She would have liked to see the look on her face.

But the consequences were not worth that small moment of satisfaction. Her mother would have asked her all sorts of awkward questions, and jumped to all the wrong conclusions.

No, it was much better this way.

Once out onto the road, Lisa glanced across at the copy of *The Scales of Justice* lying on the passenger seat. She could not wait to get home and read it. Not the whole book, unfortunately. She wouldn't have time for that. Not if she was to be perfectly groomed when Jack picked her up at six.

But she could surely manage a few chapters whilst she was soaking in the bath.

Lisa was anxious to find out just how much Hal was like Jack. He'd said on the phone last night how he liked to be prepared. Well, Lisa was going to be prepared too. For him.

CHAPTER SEVEN

As Jack drove up Tumbi Umbi Road, he started thinking it had been a long time since he'd looked forward to a date as much as he was looking forward to tonight.

Though tonight was not quite like any date he'd ever been on before. He had no expectation of ending up in bed with Lisa Chapman. In fact, he would put his money on that *not* happening.

His goal this evening was simply to get her to go out with him again. To make her see that she could have a social life without endangering her son's moral standards. That she didn't have to live like a nun, just because her husband had passed away and she didn't want to marry again.

Jack still had no idea whether Lisa had loved the man, or loathed him. But he aimed to find that out tonight as well.

A tricky mission, however, he appreciated. Because Lisa was not the sort of woman who confided easily. She kept her own counsel. Look how she hadn't told him she owned Clean-in-a-Day. That had been very secretive of her.

Still, a few glasses of wine might loosen her tongue.

There was always a lot of toasting at these award dinners. Surely she wouldn't say no to a glass or two of champagne.

The large roundabout came up that Lisa had told him about, then the street on the left she'd said to take. Shortly he'd be there, at her house.

A quick glance at his Rolex showed Jack it was one minute to six. Punctuality was one habit from the army which he'd never shaken. As was wearing his hair cut very short.

He did manage to go a few days without shaving occasionally. But that was as sloppy as he could manage. He'd been sporting quite a bit of stubble yesterday, however, something which he'd thought afterwards might not have found favour with the very particular Mrs Chapman.

But his chin was as smooth as silk tonight. So was his very expensive tuxedo, which he'd had made to measure a couple of years back.

Jack hoped his more sophisticated look would spark some sexual interest this evening. Most women liked men in dinner suits.

Unfortunately, Lisa was not most women. She was different. *Very* different.

Challenging, that was what she was.

Jack smiled as he turned down her street. There was nothing that excited him more than a challenge.

* * *

At five to six, Lisa had been close to panic. Nothing had gone as she'd planned this afternoon. Everything had taken simply ages!

Longest had been the applying of some false tan, necessary because the dress she'd bought was a one-shouldered style which showed a white strap mark. A tedious task in itself. But first, she'd had to bathe and shave her legs and exfoliate properly.

Absolutely no time for lying back and reading.

By the time all that was done to her satisfaction, it was after three. After a hurried snack, she tackled her hair, a time-consuming job as well. Again, probably because of nerves, the style she'd chosen to suit her very feminine dress just didn't work out. In the end she shampooed her hair a second time and started from scratch again, this time putting it up into a French pleat, which she could have done in her sleep. But she was disappointed and frustrated that she couldn't manage the softer, curlier look she'd wanted.

By this stage it was ten past five, leaving her less than an hour to do her nails and make-up and get dressed. The nails she managed without smudging, but it took twenty minutes. Transforming her naturally pretty face into something much more glamorous and sophisticated took another fifteen.

Foundation first, then blusher, then powder, then eyeshadow; smoky grey colours which deepened her cornflower-blue eyes. Her hand had started shaking as she applied her eye-liner, Lisa muttering some uncharacteristic swearwords when she poked herself in the eye.

Her mouth came last, with Lisa waffling over which

lipstick to use. And what colour. Her full lips didn't really need to be made to look bigger. Lisa hated that bee-stung look. In the end, she just rubbed in some lip-gloss with her fingertips.

Deciding what earrings to wear wasted another five minutes, her more severe hair-do crying out for some-thing glamorous, not the simple pearl drops she'd been planning on wearing.

Unfortunately, glamorous hadn't been on Lisa's shopping list for some years. In desperation she dragged out some long, dangling gold ones Greg had bought for her one Christmas, also changing her cream high heels for open-toed gold sandals which hadn't seen the light of day for yonks either.

Just as well they weren't a style which dated.

By then it was ten to six. Time to get into her dress.

Stripping off her bathrobe, Lisa carefully slipped the dress over her head, sliding her left arm through the one armhole whilst protecting her hair with her free hand. The dress slithered down her body, the shoulder strap halting its progress. Lisa did up the cleverly hidden side-zip, slipped her feet into her sandals then walked over to inspect the final product in the full-length mirror which hung on the back of her bedroom door.

This was where the panic set in. Instead of looking ultra-sophisticated and coolly glamorous, she looked… well…she looked sexy!

Lisa could not believe it. The dress in itself wasn't sexy. Just a chiffon sheath which skimmed her slender figure, the material graduating from cream at the top to a coffee colour down at the handkerchief hemline.

Unfortunately, the one-shouldered style meant she either had to wear a strapless bra or no bra. Given that the dress was fully lined and Lisa didn't have large breasts, she'd decided on the no-bra option. She'd always hated strapless bras, which had a tendency to slip.

She hadn't realised till this moment that her nipples would be so obvious. Or that she might look as if she had not a stitch on underneath.

Of course, she *was* wearing panties. But they were the sleek, stretchy kind which didn't show a line underneath your clothes.

Lisa was about to rummage through her underwear drawer in search of a strapless bra when she heard the sound of a car coming down the street.

Too late, she realised when it throttled down outside her house.

Grabbing her cream clutch bag, she dashed over to her bedroom window, which overlooked the street below. The sight of a sleek black sports car parked next to her post-box made her groan. The neighbours were going to have a field-day if they saw her getting into that!

She was about to run downstairs and make a quick exit when the driver's door opened and Jack climbed out.

At least, Lisa presumed it was Jack. The male who'd emerged and was currently striding up to her front door *was* remotely similar to the man she'd met the previous day. He did have the same nicely shaped head. And the same short, dark hair.

But that was where the similarity ended.

'Oh, my,' Lisa said in a soft, uncharacteristically breathy voice.

By the time he disappeared under the front porch, Lisa was shaking her head. Who would have believed that a change of clothes—and a shave—could make that much of a difference? Jack now looked just like his car. Sleek and powerful and sexy.

Sexy?

Lisa was taken aback. Since when did she start thinking any man was sexy?

Whirling away from the window, she marched off in the direction of downstairs, reminding herself the whole way down that being superficially attracted to a man was just that. Superficial.

She'd been attracted to Greg, who'd been a very handsome man. But she still hadn't liked sex with him.

Nothing has changed, she warned herself, *so don't start hoping that it has.*

The front doorbell rang on the way downstairs, Lisa's wayward thoughts back in check by the time she reached for the door knob. There were still some butterflies in her stomach over the evening ahead, but she had every confidence she could hide those. She'd been hiding her anxious nature for years.

Jack appreciated, the instant she opened the door, why he hadn't been able to get Lisa out of his mind all day.

He'd dated a lot of blondes in his time, as Helene had pointed out. But none had ever exuded what this one did.

She reminded Jack of an Alfred Hitchcock heroine. Lovely to look at. Sexy, in an understated way. But so icily self-contained that you wanted to reach out and pull her into your arms. Wanted to break her down. Wanted to make her lose her much prided self-control.

Her smile was polite. But her eyes remained annoyingly unreadable as they swept over him. 'My, don't you look simply splendid? Like James Bond on his way to a casino.'

It was a type of compliment, he supposed.

'And you look like Grace Kelly, in *To Catch a Thief*,' he countered.

Only with less underwear, he suddenly noticed.

Actually, if Jack hadn't known better, he might have thought she was totally naked underneath her dress. She certainly wasn't wearing a bra.

What he wouldn't give to reach out right now and slip that thin strap off her shoulder. In his mind's eye the dress was already slithering down her delicious body onto the doorstep, leaving her standing there wearing not much more but those sexy gold shoes.

When his own body began to respond to his mental fantasy, Jack forced himself to get a grip, clearing his throat and adopting what he hoped was a gentlemanly expression before reefing his eyes back up to her extremely beautiful face.

Her sudden blush startled him.

Because ice princesses didn't blush. They accepted compliments with cool little smiles. Their cheeks didn't go a bright red. Their composure was rarely rattled.

But Lisa was definitely rattled at that moment.

How interesting.

'Thank you,' she returned, confusion in her eyes, as

though she was well aware she was not acting like her normal self.

Even more interesting.

'Are you ready?' he asked, quite pleased at how the evening was going so far. Who knew? He might not have to be super-patient after all. If he wasn't mistaken, his little ice princess was already on the thaw.

Ready?

No, Lisa suddenly wanted to scream at him. No, I'm not ready. Not ready at all! I need a few minutes to find myself again. To find control. And composure. And to work out what happened when you looked me up and down just now.

Lisa was no stranger to men staring at her. She was used to hot, desire-filled glances. Even lecherous ogling.

Jack's gaze, however, had not been at all lecherous. His eyes had betrayed nothing but a natural interest in her appearance. In truth, Lisa would have been piqued if he hadn't complimented her.

What had upset her was her own reaction when he'd looked her up and down. Her skin had burned under the silky lining of her dress, her nipples tightening in a most disgraceful fashion.

She'd felt naked before him. Naked, and excited.

Yes, excited. That was what she'd felt.

No wonder she'd blushed.

'Have you got your house keys with you?' Jack prodded when she made no sign of moving.

'What? Oh. Yes. Yes, I think so.' She opened the gold clasp on her bag and made a pretext of inspecting its contents. 'Yes. They're here.'

'Lock up, then, and let's get going. I don't like being late.'

Lisa used the few seconds it took to lock up to calm herself. But any headway she'd made was obliterated when Jack took her arm and started steering her down the front path towards his car.

Such a simple gesture. A gentlemanly gesture, really. But the moment his large palm cupped around her elbow, electric currents went charging up and down her arm, making Lisa stiffen all over.

She smothered a sigh of relief when he let her arm go to open the passenger door of his car, grateful when he allowed her to settle herself into the seat, unaided. But she could feel his eyes on her bare legs as she swung them inside, once again making her hotly aware of her semi-naked body underneath her clothes.

She clutched her bag in her lap as he swung the door shut after her, keeping her eyes steadfastly ahead, resisting the temptation to glance up at him, for fear of what he might see in her face. But when he came into view through the front windscreen, striding round the low front of his car, Lisa surrendered to the temptation to gaze openly at him, her thoughts reflecting her ongoing shock at how he was affecting her tonight.

Just before he opened the door and climbed in behind the wheel Lisa wrenched her eyes away, hopeful he hadn't noticed her staring at him.

But what if he had?

Embarrassment curled her stomach. Please don't let him have noticed. Please let me get through this evening without making a fool of myself.

Because that was what Lisa was suddenly feeling like. A fool. Not a frigid fool any longer. Just a fool.

CHAPTER EIGHT

Jack frowned as he gunned the engine. Talk about one step forward and three steps backwards.

For a split-second, when she'd blushed, he'd thought she was warming to him.

But just when Jack had started counting his chickens, the hatching had ground to a halt. She'd acted like a marble statue when he'd taken her arm. And now she was staring out of the passenger window and clutching that bag in her lap as if she was scared stiff he was about to pounce.

Clearly, he hadn't hidden his desire for her as well as he thought he had.

Time to calm her fears with some distracting conversation, or this evening was going to be a total disaster.

'Very nice place you've got there, Lisa,' he said as he executed a U-turn and accelerated away. 'It's a credit to you.'

Her head turned and there was no mistaking the relief in her eyes. Obviously, she didn't mind his complimenting her house.

'I do like keeping it nice,' she said. 'But my mother says I'm too house-proud.'

'Nothing wrong with being house-proud. Have you always lived here?'

'Ever since my marriage. Though it looked like I'd lose the house for a while after Greg died. His insurance payout didn't cover the mortgage.'

'So what did you do?'

'I couldn't go out to work. I had a child and I hadn't booked him into childcare. So I took in ironing and cleaned houses whilst people were at work. Anywhere where I was allowed to take Cory with me. I worked seven days a week. By the time I started my business, I was close to paying off the mortgage. I'm now free and clear of debt.'

'Wow. That's impressive, Lisa.'

She shrugged those slender shoulders of hers. 'I did what I had to do. But what about you? Where did you live before you bought up here?'

'In Sydney's eastern suburbs. I still have an apartment in Double Bay. But I was finding it hard to write there. I bought the place in Terrigal as a kind of writer's retreat.'

'You must be very wealthy.'

'I've been lucky.'

'I don't believe that. People make their own luck. I'll bet writing is hard work.'

'It's becoming more so with time. When I first left the army, the words seemed to just flow.'

'Oh, so you *were* in the army. My mother said you must have been. She said you knew too much about weapons not to have handled them yourself. Once I thought about it, I agreed with her.'

'I was in the army for twelve years. Joined when I was eighteen. Left when I was thirty. I'd had enough.'

'How long ago was that?'

'Six years. Do I look thirty-six?' he asked, slanting her a quick smile. 'Or older?'

She stared back at him for a few seconds. 'Thirty-six looks about right,' she said at last. 'Though I wouldn't have been surprised if you'd been older. You do have years of experience in your eyes.'

Jack nodded. 'Some days I feel a hundred. I saw lots of things I'd rather not have seen in the army, I can tell you.'

'Hal is you, Jack, isn't he?' she suddenly said, her eyes still on him.

'He's only part me. I'm not a one-man instrument of justice and vengeance. I certainly don't go round killing people.'

'But you'd like to.'

Jack laughed. 'How perceptive of you.'

'Hal's rather ruthless.'

'He is,' Jack agreed as he negotiated the first of a series of roundabouts which would lead them past the Tuggerah shopping centre where she'd been this morning, then onto the motorway to Sydney.

'Do you think you'll win the award tonight?' Lisa asked him once they were on the motorway.

'Probably.'

'You don't sound like you really care.'

'The novelty of winning awards wears off pretty quickly.'

'That sounded cynical.'

'I *am* cynical. But awards sometimes translate into more money. And money I like. So does my agent.'

'Do you have to have an agent to become successful as a writer?'

'You do if you want to make it overseas. And especially if you want your books to be made into movies.'

'Your books are going to be made into movies?'

No doubt, that surprised her.

'They already have been. The first one premières in Los Angeles in April next year. I've been invited to attend as a special guest.'

'Wow! That's fabulous, Jack. Who's playing the part of Hal?'

'An unknown actor. The studio didn't want a big name. They wanted the person who played the part to really become Hal in people's minds. His name is Chad Furness. I hear he's very good. And very handsome.'

'Well, Hal's very handsome, isn't he? Oh, you must be so proud.'

Proud.

Jack thought about that word for a long moment.

Proud.

No. That wasn't what he felt.

Satisfied, perhaps. But not proud.

'It's certainly made me a very rich man,' came his considered reply. 'I bought this car and my penthouse at Terrigal with some of the money Hollywood paid me. Plus I hired myself a cleaner from the top cleaning establishment on the coast,' he added with a wry grin.

She laughed, the sound reassuring Jack. He would

hate to think she felt tense in his company. And she had been, earlier on.

Suddenly, the thought of never seeing her again after this evening was unbearable.

'I suppose I can't talk you into cleaning my study this Monday, could I?' he said, doing his best to sound very casual. 'Gail's ankle wouldn't have recovered yet and my study's crying out for a thorough cleaning.'

When she didn't answer, he glanced over at her.

'At the risk of being accused of trying to buy you, I'll pay you double,' he said. *And a million dollars if you'll sleep with me*, came the added Hal-like thought.

Her head turned, her eyes betraying the most intriguing dilemma. She wanted to do as he asked. He could see it. But she was hesitant. Which meant what? She did like him, but was afraid of him for some reason? Clearly, she was still worried that he was going to pounce, sexually.

'I…I can't, Jack. I have other work to do on Monday.'

'Tuesday, then.' He had no intention of letting her off the hook that easily.

'I'll send someone else.'

'No,' he snapped. 'I don't want anyone else. I want you.'

Jack could have bitten his tongue out. He'd done it now. Showed his hand. He could feel her eyes on him. Feel her tension welling up again.

'You're the best cleaner I've ever had,' he went on, hoping it wasn't too late to salvage the situation. 'You leave Gail for dead. It's difficult to go back to second rate when you've experienced perfection.'

'You're being persuasive again,' she said.

'Is it my fault if you're perfect?'

'Don't flatter me, Jack.'

'The truth is not flattery.'

'You have a way with words.'

'You have a way with floors.'

Her laugh delighted him. And made him want to roar in relief.

'All right,' she said. 'I'll clean your study. Once. On Tuesday. But after that, you're back to Gail.'

'Oh, cruel woman.'

'Stop it, Jack,' she said, but smilingly.

After that she seemed much more relaxed, and they chatted away about all sorts of things. Music. Movies. Their families. Or lack of them. Lisa's parents were divorced, and, like himself, she had no siblings. All their grandparents had passed away, too.

In a way, they were both loners. Both self-sufficient.

Occasionally, she brought the topic of conversation back to his writing. But Jack managed to steer her away from further discussion of his books, or his so-called hero.

Jack didn't want to think about Hal too much tonight. Hal could sometimes be bad for him. He appealed to his dark side. It was difficult enough ignoring the sexual thoughts and feelings Lisa could so easily evoke without Hal getting into his head, tempting him with truly wicked ideas.

Would *two* million tempt her to sleep with him? *Five?* Ten?

Jack clenched his jaw-line, then concentrated on keeping their casual conversation going, forcing himself not to fall broodingly silent as he could do on occasion when his thoughts turned dark. Which they were on the verge of doing every time he glanced over at Lisa.

Damn, but he wanted her!

His body was rock-hard with desire, his resolve to have her threatening to turn more ruthless with each passing minute.

'Not far to go now,' he said with some relief as they approached the harbour bridge. Best get out of this confining car and into somewhere public.

The traffic was a bit heavy across the bridge, but moving along steadily. Jack knew where he was going, taking the correct lanes and exit to whiz them down to the harbourside restaurant where the awards dinner was being held. Thankfully the restaurant had a private car park, reserved for patrons, an attendant swiftly directing them to a spot just metres from the entrance.

'I'd better warn you about Helene before you meet her,' he said as he extracted his car keys.

'Helene? Who's Helene?' Lisa asked.

'My agent. She's a darling woman underneath her tough-bird exterior. But she does have a big mouth. Puts her foot into it occasionally. She's also going through a gypsy-cum-gothic stage in her wardrobe, which can be a bit startling. If she'd dressed me tonight I'd have been wearing black leather trousers, with a full-sleeved white silk shirt, topped off with a scarlet cummerbund. I'd have looked like a camp pirate from the Caribbean.'

Lisa laughed, her lovely blue eyes sparkling with amusement. 'If there's one thing you could never look,

Jack, it's camp. But I'm glad this Helene didn't dress you tonight. What you're wearing is superb. That suit must have cost a small fortune.'

'It did. And I would think that little number you have on didn't come cheap. I wish you'd let me pay for it, Lisa. You shouldn't be out of pocket because you did me the favour of being my pretend girlfriend for the night.'

CHAPTER NINE

LISA found herself piqued by that word, *pretend*.

Yet she should have been reassured.

So why wasn't she?

Female vanity, she supposed. Or was it something else, that faint hope she'd been harbouring that at last she was becoming a normal woman, sexually?

During the drive down, that startling incident with her nipples had stayed at the back of her mind, as had the heat which Jack had generated in her when he'd taken her arm. Despite finally relaxing in his company and enjoying their conversation very much, she'd begun secretly hoping that he *would* make a pass when he brought her home, just to see how she would react.

The word 'pretend' indicated that Jack wasn't about to try anything. His insistence that she come and clean his study had not been a sign of personal interest. He just wanted his study cleaned. He didn't fancy her one bit.

Lisa wished now she'd accepted his offer to pay her double.

Paying for her dress, however, was still out of the question.

'Don't start that again, Jack,' she said with a cool glance his way.

The trouble with practised womanisers, she decided, was that women fell easily for their superficial charms.

When Jack came round to open the passenger door and reach his hand down towards her, Lisa smothered a groan of dismay.

There really was no option but to accept his help. Still, Lisa delayed as long as possible, swinging her feet out of the car first, her bag clutched tightly in her left hand. Finally, she put her clammy right hand into his outstretched palm, plastering a plastic smile on her face as she glanced up into his.

'Thank you,' she said with stiff politeness whilst her heart hammered away behind her ribs.

'My pleasure,' he returned, his fingers closing tightly around hers as he pulled her up onto her feet.

Lisa had a few seconds of respite when he dropped her hand and attended to locking up the car. But no sooner had she managed to calm her pulse rate a little than he slid his arm around her waist.

Naturally, she froze.

'Don't panic,' he murmured. 'Just window-dressing.'

Just window-dressing, Lisa thought almost bitterly as he propelled her towards the restaurant door. What an apt phrase to describe her! For years she'd acted like a mannequin, designed and dressed to look attractive, but not a flesh and blood woman.

No wonder Jack didn't fancy her.

'Jack! Jack!'

The owner of the voice came rushing over to them, a tall, skinny, black-haired woman dressed in the weirdest black clothes. There were lots of layers and beads, and her make-up was extremely pale and heavy, except for her bright red lipstick. Once closer, Lisa could see she was at least in her fifties.

'Helene,' Jack muttered under his breath. 'Have patience.'

'So!' The agent's beady black eyes glittered as she looked Lisa up and down. 'I knew you wouldn't come alone. Not Jack Cassidy.'

'I decided it wasn't wise to go into the lion's den without a shield by my side,' he said drily.

Helene cackled. 'It's a bit like that with you at these dos, isn't it? You're a brave woman, love,' she directed at Lisa. 'Our Jack here gets swamped by fans wanting his autograph. And a lot more of him if they can get it,' she added with a wicked wink.

'I can imagine,' Lisa replied somewhat ruefully.

Helene laughed. 'Jack, do introduce me to this delightful creature.'

'This delightful creature is Lisa, Helene. Lisa, this is Helene, my brilliant agent.'

'Heavens to Betsy! A compliment as well as a classy girlfriend! My cup runneth over! Hello, my love,' she directed at Lisa. 'You're going to wow them in the States. You are taking her with you next year, Jack. Don't tell me you're not or I'll have a pink fit right here and now.'

'I'd love to take her with me,' Jack said, pulling Lisa even closer to his side. 'But Lisa has a company to run and a son to raise. I don't think she can get away for a trip to the States, can you, darling?'

Lisa knew it was just pretend. Just window-dressing. Especially the darling bit.

But from the moment Jack's side pressed hard against hers, everything inside her began to go to mush.

'I'll have to see,' she heard herself say whilst she struggled to stop the amazing meltdown which was currently threatening her entire body.

'Make her go with you, Jack,' Helene insisted.

'I'm afraid I can't make Lisa do anything she doesn't want to do,' he said with a wry laugh. 'She's very strong-willed.'

Lisa almost laughed as well. Rather hysterically.

'Do what Hal did in your second book, Jack,' Helene advised. 'Kidnap the girl and keep her your prisoner till she says yes to everything you want.'

'I just might do that. But first, shall we go inside? Helene, look after Lisa for me for a couple of minutes, will you?'

'Will do,' the agent replied. 'Come along, lovely Lisa. We'll go in and find our table. I did ask for one of the smaller ones, knowing Jack's distaste for making idle conversation with people he cares nothing for. Hopefully, we're not stuck in some ghastly corner.'

They weren't stuck in some ghastly corner. There were no real corners, the main body of the restaurant being semicircular, with huge windows overlooking the harbour. They had, probably, *the* best table in the house, very close to a window, with a great view of the bridge *and* the opera house. The table itself was round,

covered in a crisp white tablecloth with matching ser-
viettes, extremely expensive crystal glasses and a most
spectacular, candlelit centre-piece. The carpet under-
foot was a deep blue, and the overhead lighting very
subdued.

'Golly,' Lisa said in impressed tones after the *maître
d'* had departed. 'This is a fabulous place.'

'It's OK. At least they took notice of what I asked
for. Jack's going to be pleased that it's only us.'

'But the table is set for four,' Lisa pointed out.

Helene grinned. 'I told them I had a partner.'

'And you don't?'

'Lord, no! Who'd have me? I'm a selfish, opinion-
ated, ambitious bitch. On top of that, I'm skinny and
downright ugly. Always have been.'

'You are *not* ugly,' Lisa protested. 'You're very
striking-looking.'

Helene was still preening when Jack pulled out a
chair and sat down.

'I like your Lisa, Jack. Where did you meet her?'

Lisa held her breath, hoping he didn't say she was
his cleaner.

'When I bought the penthouse at Terrigal, I
employed a cleaner. Gail. Lisa owns the cleaning
company Gail works for.'

'Oh, so you've been going out for quite a while. My,
but you're a dark horse, Jack. You never mentioned
her.'

'Didn't I?'

'You know you didn't.'

'Lisa's a very private girl, aren't you, darling?' And

he leant over and gave her a light peck on her bare shoulder.

Lisa tried not to wince. Or to cry out loud. But as window-dressing went, this was a little too close to the bone, those same bones which had almost gone to jelly the last time he'd touched her and called her darling.

Her head turned and caught his eye just as his head lifted. She meant to flash him an icy warning. Instead, she just stared at him with dazed eyes.

He stared back for a long moment, then smiled, a slow, wickedly sexy smile.

Lisa swallowed, then somehow found a smile of her own.

'Jack likes to tease me,' she said through clenched teeth. 'He knows how I hate displays of affection in public.'

'Not true,' Jack said. 'She secretly loves it.' And he kissed her shoulder again.

This time, Lisa's skin broke out into goose-pimples.

'Jack, *please*,' she choked out.

His head lifted and their eyes met once more. His were unreadable, whereas she knew hers had to be full of blind panic.

'I…I have to go to the ladies',' she said with a strained smile as she got to her feet. 'If you have to order anything whilst I'm gone, you do it for me, Jack, will you?'

Jack watched her go. Watched the other men in the place watch her go, too.

'She's very beautiful, Jack,' Helene remarked. 'Divorced?'

'No, widowed.'

'Really? So young! Still, it explains quite a bit. You know, Jack, nice girls like that don't come along too often.'

'No,' Jack agreed.

'Be good to her.'

Jack would have liked to be good to her, if she'd let him. But she wouldn't. She made that clear at every turn. Yet he knew that she *was* attracted to him, despite all her contrary body language. He'd seen the truth in her eyes just now. *Felt* it in her tensely held shoulder when he kissed it.

For whatever reason, she refused to surrender to that attraction. She was afraid.

Of *him*? Jack wondered. Or of involvement of any kind?

'Don't let her get away,' Helene added wryly.

He could, of course. Let her get away.

But Jack knew he wasn't going to do that. He'd been spot-on when he'd said she secretly liked his kissing her shoulder. She had. And it had been his total undoing.

Next time, it wouldn't be her shoulder he'd kiss. And next time, she'd wouldn't find it so easy to escape.

'Have you ordered any drinks yet?' he asked Helene abruptly.

'No, I was waiting for you.'

'I think the occasion calls for champagne, don't you?' He snapped his fingers, a waiter materialising by his side in moments. 'A magnum of your best champagne.'

'Certainly, sir.'

'A magnum!' Helen exclaimed. 'Thank heavens I came in a taxi!'

And thank heavens Lisa hadn't, Jack thought with ruthless resolve. She'd come with him.

And she'd be going home with him.

He would not break his word tonight. But he would claim a kiss goodnight at her door.

A lot could be achieved with the right kind of kiss. Jack didn't aim to stop till her eventual surrender was assured. By the time she returned to him on Tuesday on the pretext of cleaning his study, it would just be a matter of time.

Yes, indeed, he vowed darkly as he watched her weave her way through the tables back towards him, that floaty dress clinging to her body in several tantalising places. She was going to be his.

And soon.

CHAPTER TEN

Lisa had given herself a solid lecture in the ladies' room, reminding herself sternly that *she'd* made the decision to come here this evening as Jack's pretend girlfriend. It wasn't *his* fault that her hormones had suddenly come to life.

OK, so it had been a shock after all these years, to want a man the way she did Jack. And somewhat disappointing that he didn't want her back. But that was life, wasn't it? She was here now. The restaurant was lovely, the food and wine were sure to be excellent and so was the company. All she had to do was relax and enjoy herself.

An hour later, Lisa was doing just that. Amazing what a few glasses of champagne could achieve! She felt not one iota of tension. She'd become a totally different woman, tucking into her meal with gusto, not worrying over calories as she usually did. Not worrying over anything.

Conversation flowed easily from her lips whilst the champagne continued to flow past them. She even dared to flirt with Jack a little. And he flirted right back. Quite outrageously, really.

Lisa knew it was just an act. But she no longer cared. It was fun. He was fun. The evening was fun.

Whenever female fans sought him out—and after Jack won the Golden Gun award, there were quite a few of those—Jack made a big show of introducing her as his girlfriend, often giving her another of those provocative kisses, either on her shoulder or on her cheek. By then she'd long stopped freezing up, behaving in an almost cavalier way in her response to his attentions.

That she was seriously intoxicated did not cross Lisa's mind. Nothing serious crossed her mind. She felt happy for once. Genuinely happy.

Or so she deluded herself.

Coffee arrived, as did some more female fans. Three of them, all carrying copies of Jack's prize-winning book, all gushing over him as he signed them. Helene was, at that moment, away at another table, talking business to people she knew in the publishing world.

Jack went through his usual spiel of introducing Lisa as his girlfriend, this time picking up her hand and lifting it towards his mouth.

'Isn't she lovely?' he said just before his lips made contact.

If his fans said anything in reply, Lisa didn't hear it. Her focus was entirely on what Jack was doing to her hand. He wasn't just kissing it. He was making love to it, his index finger stroking the soft skin of her palm whilst his mouth moved sensually over the back of her hand, his tongue-tip leaving a wet trail as it worked its way down her middle finger.

By the time he reached the fingertip, her skin had broken out into goose-pimples. When she went to pull her hand away, his hand tightened around hers, making it impossible for her to free herself without struggling. His lips parted over the tip, sucking it slightly into his mouth.

'Jack, *really*,' she reprimanded, throwing a desperate smile at the goggle-eyed fans.

But all they did was swoon.

His head immediately lifted.

'Yes, my darling?' he enquired in a low, thickish voice.

He'd been calling her darling all evening. Up till this point, Lisa had accepted his endearment as part of the game. Part of the pretence. Suddenly, nothing felt like pretence. His eyes, usually so hard and so cool, had darkened to a smoky grey, his eyelids heavy with what looked like desire. If she wasn't badly mistaken, he wanted to make love to her for real. And not just to her hand.

'We're…we're not alone,' she pointed out, her voice shaking.

His eyes cleared abruptly as he smiled over at his by now blushing female fans.

'Forgive me,' he said, and nonchalantly dropped her hand. 'But it's not really my fault. She does dreadful things to me.'

They forgave him, of course. But could she, for acting that well? For a moment there…

'Could you take me home, please, Jack,' she said once they were gone.

'Are you serious?'

'I'm tired.' Tired of you kissing me and calling me darling. Tired of being your pretend girlfriend.

'Very well,' he said sharply, standing up and sweeping up his award in one motion.

She picked up her bag and stood up too, swaying till Jack clamped a firm hand around her elbow for support. She hadn't realised till that moment just how much champagne she'd consumed. She'd have a colossal hangover in the morning, her first in years.

Thinking about her alcohol consumption brought his to her mind.

'Are you fit to drive?' she asked.

'I'm always fit to drive.'

'You know what I mean.'

'You and Helene drank most of the champagne, Lisa. Not me.'

'Oh. I didn't notice. Shouldn't we go and say goodbye to Helene?' she said shakily when Jack urged her forward.

'She'll know where we've gone.'

He steered her from the restaurant with impolite speed, brushing off people who tried to congratulate him.

Lisa cringed with embarrassment.

'Do you know you can be very rude?' she informed him heatedly once they reached his car.

'Yes,' he threw back at her as he wrenched open the passenger door. 'It's one of my many flaws. As is arrogance and presumption. Get in, please.'

She scrambled into the passenger seat, and was still sitting there, wide-eyed with confusion, when he climbed in behind the wheel and tossed his award over into the back.

'Don't look at me like that,' he commanded after yanking his door shut and stabbing his car key into the ignition.

'Like what?'

'Like a hurt animal. If I've offended you tonight, then I'm sorry. I genuinely thought you might enjoy a night out, along with some male company. Clearly, I was wrong.'

'You weren't wrong. I did enjoy myself.'

He shook his head frustratedly at her. 'More mixed messages, Lisa? Is that a game you like to play with men? Turn them on, then turn on them?'

'I have no idea what you're talking about. You were the one kissing my shoulder and sucking on my finger. I didn't do a thing!'

'You were *liking* it,' he muttered, leaning over and putting his face so close to hers she could feel his hot breath on her skin.

'Don't,' she cried when he snaked a hand around her throat, his thumb pad tipping her chin up so that her mouth was breathtakingly close to his.

'Don't what? Don't call your bluff?'

'No, I—'

His kiss cut off any further protest, blanking her mind to everything but the feel of his mouth on hers.

It had been some years since Lisa had been kissed. She vaguely recalled liking Greg's kisses at first, till she knew where they invariably led. After that, she hadn't enjoyed them at all, her lips always remaining still and unresponsive under her husband's mouth.

Not so under Jack's.

Her lips moved restlessly against his, then parted, inviting him in. She moaned when he accepted that invitation, his tongue sliding between her teeth. She moaned again when his tongue-tip touched hers. Moaned a third time when his mouth abruptly abandoned her.

'Is this what you're afraid of?' he growled as he stared down at her flushed face. 'And why you don't date? Because you might lose some of that precious control you seem to value above everything?'

'You don't understand,' she cried.

'Don't understand what?'

'Anything.'

'Then explain it to me. Tell me what it is I don't understand.'

'I don't like sex,' she blurted out. 'That's why I don't date. Because men always want sex and I…I hate it.'

His eyebrows shot up. '*Hate* it. That wasn't hate, honey, which I felt and heard just now. You didn't want me to stop. I could have you tonight, if I wanted to.'

'You could *not*!' she exploded, pushing him back into his own seat. 'You certainly are an arrogant and presumptuous man, Jack Cassidy. Now take me home. And don't you dare touch me again, do you hear?'

'I hear you, but I don't believe you. Think about your attitude on the drive home, Lisa, and we'll talk when we get there. Because for a girl who doesn't like sex, you sure as hell liked me kissing you just now.'

'Kissing is just kissing,' she pronounced self-righteously. 'Intercourse is something else.'

* * *

GET FREE BOOKS and FREE GIFTS WHEN YOU PLAY THE...

Lucky 7

Just scratch off the silver box with a coin. Then check below to see the gifts you get!

SLOT MACHINE GAME!

YES!

I have scratched off the silver box. Please send me the 2 free Harlequin Presents® books and 2 free gifts for which I qualify. I understand I am under no obligation to purchase any books, as explained on the back of this card.

306 HDL EF37   **106 HDL EF4Y**

FIRST NAME	LAST NAME

ADDRESS

APT.#	CITY

STATE/PROV.	ZIP/POSTAL CODE

7	7	7	**Worth TWO FREE BOOKS plus 2 BONUS Mystery Gifts!**
🍒	🍒	🍒	**Worth TWO FREE BOOKS!**
♣	♣	♣	**Worth ONE FREE BOOK!**
🔔	🔔	🍒	**TRY AGAIN!**

www.eHarlequin.com

(H-P-12/06)

Offer limited to one per household and not valid to current Harlequin Presents® subscribers.

Your Privacy - Harlequin Books is committed to protecting your privacy. Our Privacy Policy is available online at www.eHarlequin.com or upon request from the Harlequin Reader Service. From time to time we make our lists of customers available to reputable firms who may have a product or service of interest to you. If you would prefer for us not to share your name and address, please check here ☐.

The Harlequin Reader Service® — Here's how it works:

Accepting your 2 free books and 2 free mystery gifts places you under no obligation to buy anything. You may keep the books and gifts and return the shipping statement marked "cancel." If you do not cancel, about a month later we'll send you 6 additional books and bill you just $3.80 each in the U.S., or $4.47 each in Canada, plus 25¢ shipping & handling per book and applicable taxes if any.* That's the complete price and — compared to cover prices of $4.50 each in the U.S. and $5.25 each in Canada — it's quite a bargain! You may cancel at any time, but if you choose to continue, every month we'll send you 6 more books, which you may either purchase at the discount price or return to us and cancel your subscription.

*Terms and prices subject to change without notice. Sales tax applicable in N.Y. Canadian residents will be charged applicable provincial taxes and GST. All orders subject to approval. Credit or debit balances in a customer's account(s) may be offset by any other outstanding balance owed by or to the customer. Please allow 4 to 6 weeks for delivery.

If offer card is missing write to: Harlequin Reader Service, 3010 Walden Ave., P.O. Box 1867, Buffalo NY 14240-1867

BUSINESS REPLY MAIL

FIRST-CLASS MAIL   PERMIT NO. 717-003   BUFFALO, NY

POSTAGE WILL BE PAID BY ADDRESSEE

HARLEQUIN READER SERVICE
3010 WALDEN AVE
PO BOX 1867
BUFFALO NY 14240-9952

NO POSTAGE
NECESSARY
IF MAILED
IN THE
UNITED STATES

Intercourse?

Jack stared over at Lisa. Was this girl for real? Did she live in the twenty-first century?

There were lots of words used to describe the sex act these days. But intercourse was rarely one of them. It was as outdated as beautiful young blondes not liking sex.

'How many men have you been to bed with?' he demanded to know before he drove anywhere.

'I don't have to tell you that.'

'You were a virgin when you got married, weren't you?'

'No,' she replied defensively. 'I was not.'

'So how many cretin lovers have you had?'

'None. One. I mean…Greg was *not* a cretin!'

'You've only ever been with your husband? I thought you said you weren't a virgin when you got married.'

'We slept with each other before we were married.'

'I see. And you never enjoyed sleeping with him?'

'No.'

'Then why in heaven's name did you marry him?'

'You don't understand! I…I needed to get married. To have my own home. My own family. Greg was a good man. And I loved him.'

'But you weren't *in* love with him. If you were, you'd have liked anything he did to you. Even if you didn't come, you'd have liked the lovemaking. And the intimacy.'

Lisa's old nemesis, guilt, consumed her again. She should not have married Greg. She could see that now.

But this man—this playboy!—had no right to judge her.

Jack sighed. 'What on earth am I going to do with you?'

'You're going to take me home,' she snapped, fighting back tears.

'I don't think so. You're coming home with me.'

'I am not!'

'*Think*, Lisa,' he said, his eyes turning strangely tender. 'You're thirty years old, and you've never enjoyed sex. If you keep going the way you've been going, you'll go to your death never knowing what you've missed. I'm a good lover. A skilled lover. I know what a woman likes. Let me show you what you've been missing.'

She just stared at him, not knowing what to say. Or what to do.

She was tempted. Of course she was tempted.

But she was also terrified.

'Don't be afraid,' he whispered, leaning over to kiss her again. Very lightly this time, sipping at her lips till they fell wantonly apart once more.

His head slowly lifted, his eyes locking with hers as his hands gently cupped her cheeks.

'You need to come home with me, Lisa. You're not a coward. You have great courage. More courage than any woman I've ever known. Take this leap of faith and trust me. I won't hurt you, I promise. I'll be good to you.'

'But you don't really fancy me!' she blurted out.

His laughter was soft and wry. 'Not fancy you? Oh, Lisa, how little you comprehend the true nature of men.

Of course I fancy you. I've fancied you since the first moment I set eyes on you.'

'But you…you…'

'Yes,' he said, nodding, 'I let you think otherwise. I confess. I'm a ruthless bastard when I want something. And I wanted you, my lovely. Now lean back and fasten your seat belt.'

'I didn't agree to come home with you!'

'Yes, you did. The last time I kissed you. Of course, you do have the right to change your mind at any stage. And to say no. Are you saying no now?'

She shook her head in the negative, her whole being suddenly consumed by a breathless excitement.

'Good,' Jack said as he gunned the engine. 'Now close your eyes and rest. You could be in for a rather long night.'

CHAPTER ELEVEN

SHE didn't close her eyes, Jack noted as he drove. She sat there with her hands clasped nervously around that infernal bag, her body language betraying an increasingly uptight state.

He put on some music in an attempt to relax her but to no avail. All she did was grip that bag tighter and stare out of the passenger window.

On Jack's part, he found his initial sense of triumph at her agreeing to come home with him soon fading to frustration. He half expected her to tell him to take her straight home as he drove down the hill from Kariong. His own knuckles were white on the steering wheel by the time he made it through West Gosford.

It took all of his will-power not to sigh with relief once he was safely on the road which led out to the beaches, and Terrigal.

But he sensed she was still worried. Or afraid. Or both.

An understanding state of mind, he supposed, given her sexual history.

She must have had a miserable marriage, poor darling.

Jack hoped she would let him show her that she didn't have to shun men and sex forever just because she'd been incompatible with one partner.

People were not machines, especially women. The chemistry had to be right on both sides for a sensitive female like Lisa to find satisfaction. She needed to desire as well as be desired.

Jack knew the chemistry between them was right. But she had to give him the chance to show her that.

By the time Jack reefed the Porsche into his driveway and shot down the side-ramp which led to the underground car-park, he had resolved to be patient, but persistent. He would not let her change her mind. Or give in to her doubts and fears.

'I can see your main problem,' he remarked as he released his seat belt. 'You think too much. What star sign are you?'

'Virgo,' she said, and he nodded.

'How come I'm not surprised? The sign of the worrier. So what have you been worrying about during the drive here?'

She turned to him, still clutching that bag as if it were a lifeline. 'I've been thinking it could have been the champagne, Jack,' she said, her tone anxious. 'That's why I liked you kissing me.'

'What are you saying exactly? You only liked me kissing you because you were drunk?'

'Yes. That's what I'm saying.'

'Do you feel drunk now?'

'No,' she said with surprise in her voice. 'Actually, my head feels quite clear.'

'I can believe that,' he pointed out drily. 'Because you're back to being all uptight again.'

Her lovely face screwed up in an expression of sheer frustration. 'I know I am. I hate it when I get like this. I really do.'

'In that case, I have a bottle of excellent white wine chilling in the fridge door. Let's go open it and get you right back to being nicely relaxed again.'

Her blue eyes widened. 'You want to get me drunk again?'

'I want you not thinking. Or worrying. If that means you have to be on the tipsy side, then yes, I do.'

Again, he could see temptation in her eyes. And that irritating fear as well.

'Come on, beautiful,' he said softly. 'I dare you to do something out of your comfort zone for once. Put the ice princess away for tonight and let me bring out the woman you've always wanted to be.'

Lisa winced at the term 'ice princess'. Was that how he saw her?

It made her angry. Because it was true. That was how lots of people saw her. Her employees. Her mother. And now Jack.

She supposed she couldn't blame them. She was the girl who turned off movies once the sex scenes started. And skipped the really raunchy parts in books.

Though never in Jack's books, Lisa suddenly realised. She always read the pages where Hal made love to a woman.

No, not made love. Hal never made love. He had sex with women. All kinds of sex.

Lisa swallowed. She hoped Jack wouldn't be expecting the sort of foreplay Hal always demanded. She would die rather than do that.

Thinking about it made her feel sick.

'I'm sorry, Jack,' she choked out, her eyes dropping to her lap. 'I can't do this.'

'Yes, you can. Look at me, Lisa!' he commanded.

She looked up at him.

'You're not drunk now, are you?'

'No.'

'Good.'

He leant over and kissed her again, a hot, hungry kiss which was as demanding as it was irresistible. She moaned softly when his tongue dipped deep into her mouth, her nipples tightening once more, her heart pounding within her chest. Soon, she wanted more than his mouth on her. She wanted his hands as well.

'No,' she cried out in confusion when his head lifted.

'I don't want to hear that word again tonight,' he replied thickly. 'It's going to be yes. To everything. Come on. Time I got you upstairs.'

She's like a virgin, Jack reminded himself as he helped her out of the car. Just look at her eyes. So wide. And innocent.

He would have to be gentle, and patient. Have to contain his own desire and think of nothing the first time but giving *her* pleasure.

He'd never done that before. Not really. Yes, he was

an accomplished lover. And yes, he knew how to satisfy
a woman. But his intentions in doing so in the past had
always been totally selfish. A well-satisfied woman
always came back for more.

Lisa, however, inspired him to be less selfish and
more gallant. Yes, of course he still wanted her to come
back for more. But that wasn't as important, suddenly,
as seeing the rapture in her eyes when she came for the
first time.

'Now, don't start thinking,' he whispered, holding
her close as he steered her over to the lift well.

'It's hard not to.'

'Every time I see you thinking I'm going to kiss
you,' he promised.

And he did. In the lift. At his front door. In the
middle of the living room. Even whilst he carried her
down to his bedroom.

By the time he lowered her down onto her feet by
his bed, her breathing was quick and her eyes dilated,
two sure signs that she was seriously turned on.

His job now was to undress her, *without* turning
her off again.

Earrings first, Jack decided, blowing softly into her
ear after he unhooked each one and dropped it on the
nearest bedside table. Her shivers were reassuring. But
he still kissed her again after the second earring had
been disposed of.

By the time his head lifted, her breathing was very fast.

'Now, how do I get you out of this dress?' he asked
softly.

Her hands were visibly shaking when they reached

up to slide down the zip which was hidden in the side-seam.

'Aah,' he said, and slowly pushed the strap off her shoulder and down her arm. The dress went too, as it had in his mental fantasy, slithering down her body before pooling on the floor at her feet.

The sudden sight of her near-naked body jolted his resolve to stay cool. Lord, but she was beautiful. Beautiful shape, beautiful skin, beautiful breasts. They were small, but quite exquisite.

She was exquisite.

No one would have believed she'd had a child. Only her nipples gave her away. They were comparatively large, and dusky coloured. And very erect, calling out to him to touch them...

'Jack,' she choked out, snapping his eyes back up to her face.

The fear was back, he saw, widening her eyes again and stiffening her shoulders.

Damn you, Jack, get your act together!

He had no option but to kiss her again. But the feel of her bare breasts pressed against his chest threatened to unravel him. When she wound her arms up around his neck and melted against him, his battle for control looked in danger of being lost.

He wrenched his mouth away, his own breathing very ragged. He had to get her away from him for a while.

He sat her down on the side of the bed, keeping his eyes averted from her breasts—and the rest of her de-licious body—whilst he removed her shoes. As a distancing ploy, it failed miserably. His hands would not obey him, sliding up her calves, caressing her knees then moving on to her by then quivering thighs.

A desire such as he'd never known gripped him, compelling him to tip her back onto the bed and remove her panties.

How he managed to ease them down her legs slowly instead of ripping them off her, he had no idea.

Just in time, he reefed his mind back from the brink, steeling himself to ignore his own increasingly desperate need and take his time with her.

But it was going to be difficult. More difficult than he'd ever imagined. She affected him, this girl, in ways he had yet to understand. If he didn't know better, he might think he was falling in love with her.

The thought startled him. Jack didn't fall in love. He *never* fell in love. He was like Hal. Dead inside. And hard.

But not with this girl. She brought out the softness in him.

She stared up at him as he rose to his feet, her eyes wide yet trusting. She was waiting for him to make love to her. *Make love*, Jack. Not have sex.

Make love to her, then, man. And do it well.

Because she deserves it.

CHAPTER TWELVE

LISA swallowed as she watched his hands go to his bow-tie, flicking it undone whilst he kicked his shoes off. His jacket followed next. Then his socks.

He was going to take everything off, she realised dazedly. Going to get naked. As naked as she was.

Why wasn't she embarrassed, lying there in front of Jack without any clothes on? Why wasn't she trying to cover herself up? Why wasn't she searching her mind for any excuse to cut and run?

She certainly had been earlier.

But that was before he'd kissed her a zillion times. And before she'd been consumed with the craving for more.

His kisses were no longer enough.

So she lay there, with a huge lump in her throat and the desperate hope that he was right and she was about to become the woman she'd always secretly wanted to be.

His shirt went the same way as his jacket and bow-tie, revealing the magnificent upper body Lisa already suspected he had. His skin was deeply tanned, a V of dark curls covering the area between his broad chest muscles, arrowing down past his washboard stomach into the waistband of his trousers...that waist band which he'd just snapped open.

Lisa found herself holding her breath as he reefed the zip down and pushed the trousers off his slim hips.

His legs were as muscular as his arms, his black briefs straining to contain his erection.

Lisa's mouth dried when they hit the floor as well.

'Let's get that quilt off,' he said with a warm smile as he walked towards the bed. 'And you up onto the pillows.'

He scooped her up as if she were a feather, holding her against him with one arm whilst he flung back the black velvet quilt with the other.

Lisa could not help thinking how she'd made this very bed yesterday, never imagining that tonight she would be sleeping in it.

Yet here she was, being lowered into the crisp white sheets, naked as the day she was born.

She shivered when Jack stretched out beside her.

'Not cold, are you?' he enquired.

'No,' she choked out. Just shockingly nervous.

'Methinks she needs some more kissing.'

His lips took a passionate possession of hers, his right hand cupping her chin and keeping her mouth captive beneath his.

Not that it needed to be kept captive. She was already addicted to Jack's kisses, loving the way he dominated her with his mouth, and his tongue.

But this was the first time he'd kissed her lying down. And the first time they'd been naked together.

The feel of his bare body pressed up against hers was

electrifying. She yearned for more contact, wanting his hands on other, more intimate places.

As though he sensed her need, his hand slid down from her chin to her breast, caressing the rock-like tip till she shuddered uncontrollably. He immediately stopped kissing her and bent down to put his mouth where his hand had been.

Lisa almost jackknifed from the bed when he sucked on her breast, the tugging sensation sending wild *frissons* of pleasure rippling down her spine. He pressed her back down with his large hand splayed wide over her stomach, and kept on sucking her nipple.

Oh, yes, she thought. Yes!

When his hand moved lower and slid between her legs, her pleasure doubled. No, *tripled!*

Jack seemed to know just where to touch to make her squirm with delight. And all the while his mouth remained on her breast, sometimes sucking, sometimes licking, sometimes taking her sensitised nipple between his teeth and tugging it ever so gently.

Soon, she wanted still more. Not his fingers. Him. She wanted *him*. How amazing! She'd never wanted a man like this before. Never wanted sex like this before. Never wanted to feel a man plunging deep into her.

Yet she wanted Jack. And she wanted him now.

'Jack,' she cried out in a voice she did not recognise.

His head lifted and their eyes met.

'Please,' she begged him. 'Please…'

'I have to get a condom, Lisa.'

'No, no, don't leave me. It's safe. I promise you it's safe.' She hadn't long finished her period. 'I can't possibly get pregnant.'

Jack would have loved to just keep going. But he hadn't exercised an iron will over his own control to lose his head now.

The fact she was so turned on pleased him no end. Hell, he couldn't have felt more thrilled. But she would hate herself afterwards if he did what she thought she wanted. She would worry about other things. She was a Virgo, after all.

Still, he could understand her desperation. There were times, especially with women, when any delay could be disastrous. She needed a climax and she needed it now.

'Close your eyes and don't think,' he ordered her brusquely.

Lisa gasped with shock when Jack slid even further down her body, once again putting his mouth where his hands had been.

Never had she allowed Greg such an intimacy with her. Never ever!

For a split-second her mind revolted, but then his lips and tongue found the right spot and she was lost to sensations which could only be described as deliciously decadent. Her body wallowed in the most primal pleasure whilst her prudish mind tried to get around all that he was doing to her down there. One part of her wanted to push him away. But the overriding part refused to obey. His mouth kept her in thrall whilst his fingers entered her, filling her, stretching her. *Tormenting* her.

Her head threshed from side to side, her mouth gaping wide as the cruellest tension gripped her body. Her chest felt like a vice around her heart, her belly tightening in a way she had never felt before. Her inner muscles followed suit, gripping Jack's fingers.

'Oh!' she cried out when the first spasm hit. Then, 'Ooooh,' as more spasms followed, exquisitely pleasurable contractions which released her from wanting anything but that they go on forever.

Unfortunately, they didn't, slowly declining in intensity till they stopped altogether.

'Oooooh,' she moaned, then went all limp and languid.

Lisa was lying there with heavy eyes and much slower breathing when Jack's face materialised above hers, his hard grey eyes quite smug.

'Good?' he said.

For a moment, embarrassment threatened to raise its spoiling head. He'd just been down there, after all, seeing and invading her with stunning intimacy.

But she refused to go back to being the woman she'd been before meeting Jack. That frigid failure of a female was about to be banished. Forever.

At the same time, Lisa could not seem to stop a hot blush from invading her cheeks.

'Now, none of that, madam,' Jack chided. 'You've done nothing to feel ashamed of. You're a normal, healthy woman who deserves a normal, healthy sex life. You've wasted too many years thinking you don't like making love. You do. You just needed the right lover. Now, don't go away, beautiful. And don't start worrying. I'll be back in a moment.'

Lisa barely had time to think before he came back. And this time, he was wearing a condom.

That Jack hadn't yet been sexually satisfied had slipped Lisa's mind. Which just showed how inexperienced she was when it came to matters in the bedroom.

'So what did you think of your first orgasm?' he asked after he'd rejoined her on the bed, startling her when he immediately began caressing her body, his fingertips running up and down her sides with long, feathery strokes.

'What? Oh…yes. It was…incredible.'

'The next one will be better.'

'The next one?'

'I did say you were in for a long night.'

'But…'

He rolled over and braced himself on his elbows above her, his erection resting high on her stomach.

'Lift your knees,' he ordered her.

She didn't even think about disobeying him. He was that sort of man.

'This should feel better than my fingers,' he said as he reached down and directed himself slowly into her.

Lisa swallowed. He was right. It felt much better than his fingers.

'Now, wrap your legs around my waist. No, higher. You know, you're amazingly tight for a woman who's had a child.'

Lisa frowned at this last statement, which showed an intimate and expert knowledge of the female body.

You're having sex with a playboy, she reminded herself, a man who's been with a lot of women in his life. Don't forget that he doesn't fall in love with them, or keep them. You're just a plaything, his latest pent-house pet. Don't ever imagine you'll be anything else.

But she still did as she was told, and he slid in even deeper, making her gasp.

'I'm not hurting you, am I?'

'No no, it's…lovely.' An understatement. It was…amazing.

He smiled. 'That's my girl.'

No, I'm not, she thought with a jolt to her potentially vulnerable heart. I'm just someone you fancy. For the moment. I'm disposable. And replaceable.

Always remember that, Lisa. Don't let him con you. Or use you.

Jack's a charming and very sexy man. But he's a practised womaniser.

The thought distressed her to a degree.

Till she got hold of her silly self again.

'Jack…'

'What?'

'Why do I like this with you? Why didn't I like it with my husband? He really wasn't that bad a lover.'

He shrugged his broad shoulders. 'Who knows? Maybe you were too young. Some women mature late, sexually. And like I said, you weren't in love with him.'

'But I'm not in love with you, either.'

'Thanks a bunch.'

'You know what I mean. I don't even know you. We only met yesterday.'

'Falling in love has nothing to do with knowing each other, Lisa. It's a physical thing, a chemistry. That's where the saying *love at first sight* comes from. Still, maybe it should be called falling in lust, not love.'

'I see. And did you fall in lust with me at first sight?' she asked, intrigued by the concept.

'Undoubtedly. Now, why don't you shut up and let me show you how much.'

His moving inside her very definitely shut her up. She wrapped her arms and ankles around his back. Soon, she felt compelled to move with him, her hips lifting. Her hands dropped back down to grab his buttocks, her nails digging in as she pulled him even deeper into her.

'If there's anything I hate,' Jack said with a raw groan, 'it's a quick learner.'

'I'm going to come, Jack,' she blurted out.

'The heavens be praised!'

If she'd thought her first climax was fabulous, this one was beyond that. It wasn't a shattering apart so much as a coming together. They cried out together, shuddered together, then found peace together, wrapped in each other's arms.

This was what making love should always be like, Lisa thought rapturously.

Her yawn came out of the blue.

'Time for a little nap, perhaps,' Jack said softly, easing himself out of her and pulling a sheet up over her shoulders.

'But I don't want to sleep,' she protested, even as she yawned again.

'Don't worry. I won't let you sleep for long.'

CHAPTER THIRTEEN

JACK watched her go to sleep, waiting till her eyelids stopped fluttering and her breathing was deep before he left her to go to the bathroom.

He just stood there, staring in the mirror, having a silent conversation with himself.

She's a very special girl, Jack. Don't you hurt her.

Of course I won't. I'll be good to her. And for her. She needed liberating from the prison of her imagined frigidity. She needs a man who can make her relax and have some fun for a change. But most of all, she needs a lot of great sex!

Jack's next mission was to show her that making love did not always have to take place in the bedroom.

But first, he'd let her sleep for a while. He might even have a reviving nap himself. Make sure he was on top of his game for the next round.

Lisa stirred to the lightest touch on her shoulder.

For a split-second, she thought it was Cory, waking her after having a bad dream. But it wasn't her son leaning over her. It was Jack.

He was sitting on the side of the bed and smiling down at her.

'Feeling refreshed?' he asked.

'What…what time is it?'

'Two-ish. You've been asleep for a couple of hours.'

'Oh,' Lisa said weakly as a whole rush of memories and emotions bombarded her.

There was still amazement over what had happened. But more than a dampening suspicion that her champagne consumption during dinner *had* played a role in making her more receptive to Jack's lovemaking. A dull thudding in her temples indicated a hangover. Even worse was the shame that she'd been so easy to seduce, after all she'd said to him.

Her only solace was that she was at his place, and not her own.

At least Cory wasn't around to witness his mother's downfall.

'Oh, no,' Jack said, wagging his finger at her. 'There'll be none of that.'

'None of what?'

'Regrets and recriminations.'

'But I *was* drunk, Jack,' she insisted, clutching the sheet up over her breasts. 'I have a splitting headache to prove it.' It was an exaggeration, she knew. But she had to find some excuse for her behaviour.

'You were not drunk. Not by the time we arrived here.'

'Then why have I got a hangover?'

'Sex can sometimes give people headaches. It's the rise in blood pressure, then the sudden relaxing. I have some painkillers in the bathroom. Stay where you are. I'll get you some.'

It wasn't till he rose from the bed and began striding over to the bathroom that she realised he was still as naked as she was.

She stared at his bare bottom, shocked by the red scratch marks on his untanned buttocks.

Did I do that?

I must have.

It was a startling realisation, evidence of a wild passion which was already becoming a hazy memory. So were her climaxes. Had they really been so mind-blowing?

Jack wasn't gone more than thirty seconds, returning with a glass of water and two tablets in his hand.

Not that she overly noticed either till he practically shoved them in her face. She'd been staring at his naked front this time. Didn't he get embarrassed, walking around like that?

'Here,' he said.

Taking the glass and tablets from him forced Lisa to drop the sheet which she'd been holding over her breasts. Their sudden exposure—along with Jack's staring down at them—made her squirm inside.

'I...I need to go to the bathroom,' she said after gulping down the tablets.

He shrugged. 'Be my guest.'

'I...I haven't got a robe.'

'You don't need one. The bathroom's just over there.'

There was a note of challenge in his voice. A kind of dare in his eyes.

Steeling herself, Lisa threw back the sheet and

swung her feet over the side of the bed. Really, it was ridiculous for her to feel so embarrassed. He'd seen more of her, after all.

But this was different somehow. Yet still strangely exciting, she had to admit. To have him watch her walk, naked, across the room. To feel his eyes following her every move.

And her knowing all the while how much he wanted her.

Was that what was making her skin flush and her heart race like mad? Her awareness of *his* desire?

Or was it her own?

Lisa shook her head as she washed her hands afterwards. What to do? Demand that he take her home? Or let him do whatever he wanted to do to her?

When she glanced up into the vanity mirror, her brilliant blue eyes showed her that there really wasn't any contest. She could not leave just yet. She had to know what more there was.

Returning to the bedroom took more courage than leaving it.

Finding it empty came as a shock. Where had Jack gone to?

When he didn't come back after a couple of minutes, Lisa had no option but to go in search of him. But not in the nude, she decided. She wasn't that brave. Or that bold.

Her clothes, however, were not on the floor where he'd dropped them before. And there was no sign of a robe anywhere. Clearly, Jack didn't wear one.

In the end she wrapped a bath-sheet around herself and padded in her bare feet down the hallway, popping her head into his study on the way. Not there. But brother, he was right. That room was seriously messy.

He wasn't in the living room, either. She found him in the kitchen, brewing coffee and making toasted sandwiches.

His having donned some black satin boxer shorts was a huge relief.

'Feeling better?' he asked with a quick smile her way.

'A bit. What happened to my dress and underwear?'

'Your dress is hanging up in my walk-in closet and your panties are currently in the washing machine. I'll pop them in the dryer shortly.'

'Oh. Thank you, but you didn't have to.'

'I thought you might enjoy someone looking after you for a change.'

Lisa didn't know what to say to that. No one had ever looked after her. She'd pretty well looked after herself when she was growing up. Plus all the time during her marriage to Greg. She'd worn the trousers in the family, right from the start. Which was the way she'd liked it. But she'd worked hard for the privilege of being the boss, doing all of the housework, controlling the money, paying all the bills.

Then, after Greg died, and she'd really been on her own, she'd had to do absolutely everything herself, even the garden. Nowadays, she paid a man to mow her lawns, but she hadn't been able to afford that at first. She'd bogged in and done it all herself, even learning how to change light bulbs and washers, jobs she'd used to delegate to Greg.

Jack smiled over at her again. 'Why don't you let your hair down?'

'What?'

'Your hair. It's come loose at the back. Here, let me do it for you.'

His moving behind her was unnerving, so were his hands in her hair. She held herself stiffly whilst he removed the hidden pins then stroked her hair down to her shoulders.

When he bent to kiss her on the shoulder, she froze some more.

'Relax,' he murmured. 'I won't bite.'

'Then stop acting like the big bad wolf,' she shot back at him.

He laughed, but moved back to what he'd been doing at the kitchen counter, leaving her annoyed with herself for being silly. She'd decided to stay, hadn't she? Why start snapping at him?

'I'm sorry, Jack,' she said, climbing up onto one of the leather-topped stools which faced the huge breakfast bar. 'That was uncalled-for.'

'No, no,' he said, grinning over at her. 'You were quite right. I *was* acting like the big bad wolf. In truth, I'd like to gobble you up right here and now. But I can wait. Hope you like melted cheese on your toast.'

'I'm not fussy,' she said, and he laughed.

'Now, that's a big fib, Miss Prissy. But I'll forgive you if you take that towel off while we eat.'

Lisa gaped at him. 'You want me to sit and eat in the nude?'

'I'm game if you're game,' he said and, pushing the

black boxer shorts down to the floor, he stepped out of them and kicked them away.

Lisa's mouth dropped further open before snapping shut. 'Why do I suspect you've done things like this before?'

'Never! Not here, anyway. I haven't brought a single woman back to this place since I bought it. I've been celibate for weeks and weeks, finishing that infernal book.'

Lisa thrilled to the thought he hadn't slept with any other woman recently. Though perhaps that was why he was pursuing her so avidly. He was seriously frustrated.

'Well?' Jack prompted, walking over to the breakfast bar with two plates of toasted sandwiches in his hands. 'I'm waiting.'

'I can't, Jack.'

'Don't be ridiculous. I won't even be able to see all of you from here. Just your top half. You're not shy about showing off your very pretty breasts, are you?'

She was suddenly shy about showing anything!

Yet she wanted to. That was the weirdest thing with Jack. He could make her want to do things that she found embarrassing.

'But you'll *know* I'm totally naked,' she protested.

'That's the point, Lisa. My *knowing*. It's a turn-on.'

'But you don't need turning on.'

'I wasn't talking about me, beautiful.'

'Oh…'

'Just do it,' he said. 'And see for yourself.'

Her heart started hammering behind her ribs even

before her hand moved to do his bidding. By the time she'd removed the towel and draped it over the stool next to her, Lisa was feeling light-headed. And hot. When Jack placed her plate and mug in front of her, she just stared blankly down at them, then up at him.

'I...I don't think I'm hungry,' she said quietly.

'You should eat something. And drink the coffee. I don't want you fainting on me.'

'I never faint.'

'There's a first time for everything.'

Yes, Lisa thought shakily. And tonight she'd experienced a lot of firsts.

If only her mother could see her now...

Thinking of her mother brought Lisa up with a jolt.

Jill Chapman had had quite a few lovers after her husband had left her, Lisa hating the times she'd come home from school to find the evidence of her mother's affairs. The extra-wet towel in the bathroom. The smell of sex in the house. Her mother's smudged lipstick and lack of underwear.

Lisa had always prided herself on being nothing like her mother in that regard.

Yet here she was, sitting naked in Jack Cassidy's kitchen, totally breathless and shockingly aroused.

The whole scenario seemed unbelievable.

'You're doing it again,' Jack growled, moving his coffee away from his lips.

'Doing what?'

'Thinking.'

'There's nothing wrong with thinking.'

'There is when *you* do it.'

'I think I should go home,' she suddenly blurted out.

His eyes darkened as he slowly lowered his coffee back down to the marble counter. 'Is that what you really want to do?'

'Yes... No... I don't know! And I don't *like* not knowing, Jack,' she cried in dismay. 'I don't like being out of control.'

He grimaced, then shook his head. 'Maybe I've gone too fast. Maybe we should leave things as they are till another day.'

Lisa blinked. 'Another day?'

His eyes were as uncompromising as the set of his mouth. 'You don't honestly think tonight is the end of us, do you?'

'Well, I...I know I promised to clean your study on Tuesday.'

'That's not what I mean and you know it.'

'But you're not into relationships,' she argued. 'I mean...you said as much up front.'

'I said I didn't want to get married. But that doesn't stop me having a girlfriend. I want you to be my girl-friend, Lisa. I want to take you places. Buy you things. Spoil you rotten.'

She just stared at him. Oh, but he was wicked.

'I *can't* be your girlfriend,' she threw at him. 'I mean...I don't *want* to be your girlfriend.'

His head jerked back as if she'd slapped him in the face. 'Might I ask why not?'

'Because I don't have the time!'

'That's bulldust. You have lots of time. You're your own boss. Tell me the truth.'

'All right. It will complicate things.'

'In what way?'

'Cory is my first priority in life. I refuse to do anything which will jeopardise his happiness.'

'How will your being my girlfriend jeopardise your son's happiness? I won't interfere in his upbringing and I'll be good to him. I'll take him places too, and buy him things. Things all boys like.'

Now he was being even more wicked. Trying to seduce her through her son. But he'd made a mistake, thinking his materialistic offer would sway her.

'That's exactly what I'm talking about. Cory will start thinking how wonderful you are. You're his kind of man, Jack. Then one day, you'll say, *Sorry, Lisa, but I'm getting bored playing father*. And that will be that. And Cory will be broken-hearted all over again. It was tough enough for him losing his dad. And he wasn't all that old then. He's nine now. He can be really hurt this time.'

'In that case, we'll keep Cory out of our relationship.'

Lisa shook her head. 'How? I have no intention of leaving Cory alone, or shipping him round to neighbours to mind. I'd have to tell my mother about us and...'

'And what's wrong with that?' Jack broke in, his face becoming more frustrated with each second.

'You don't understand!' she cried.

'No, I don't.' His hands lifted to rake agitatedly through his hair. 'We're having our first fight and we're not even going together yet. Look, why don't we just stop this and go back to bed? We get along in bed. Very nicely.'

She just stared at him, her head whirling. He wasn't going to let her say no to him again. She could see that.

'If that doesn't appeal,' he went on with a very sexy smile, 'we could go skinny-dipping in the pool and make leisurely love in the water.'

Lisa swallowed at this last thought. She'd never made love in water. Or anywhere other than in a bed.

The idea was both tantalising and tempting, exactly as Jack knew it would be. He was the devil in disguise, she decided. An accomplished seducer of women, especially silly, inexperienced women like herself.

'You choose,' Jack said, any talk of taking her home apparently overridden and forgotten.

The pool room, Lisa knew from having cleaned it, was like a decadent Roman bath-house. The walls of the room were covered in black marble tiles, the surrounds of the pool and spa in white, and the pool itself in a deep blue.

When she didn't say anything, he strode round and scooped her up off the stool.

'Don't you ever know what's good for you?' he growled as he carried her, not back to the bedroom but in the direction of the pool.

Yes, she thought with despairing insight. And it's not you, Jack Cassidy. You're a dangerous man to be with. A ruthless, charming, cold-blooded womaniser. I know you. I've read all your books. You're not the devil in disguise. You're Hal Hunter in disguise.

That man eats women for breakfast and spits them out.

But at the same time, you're the first man to make me feel like this. I can't turn my back on what you have to offer. I just can't.

But I'm going to do my level best to keep my head. I am *not* going to fall in love with you, Jack Cassidy. Absolutely and positively not!

CHAPTER FOURTEEN

'I NEVER thought I'd see you without make-up,' was her mother's first comment when Lisa arrived at her place the following day. 'Or without blow-drying your hair.'

Lisa's hands lifted to run through her hair, still damp from the second shower she'd had after Jack drove her home, and after she'd made a hurried call to her mother, saying she'd be right out. Lisa hadn't had the time—or the inclination—for hair and make-up. Her head was too full of other things.

'I was too tired to bother,' she said distractedly. 'I guess I look a mess.'

'Not at all. You look lovely. Still, you must have had a really good time to stay out so late. Come on, come inside. I want to hear every single detail.'

Lisa rolled her eyes as she followed her mother into the house. She had no intention of telling her mother any such thing.

Not because her mother would be scandalised. But because she would ask Lisa awkward questions which she had no answers for.

Never had Lisa felt so confused, or so rattled. Her life had suddenly spun out of control—as had she—and she didn't know where it would all end.

The only surety in her mind was that her affair with Jack was a long way from being over. Overnight, she'd turned into a sex maniac, totally obsessed by the man and what she felt when she was with him.

It had taken every bit of will-power she had not to agree to race over to Jack's place after dropping Cory off at school tomorrow morning. He'd certainly pressed her to do just that when he drove her home today.

She'd sounded surprisingly cool and matter-of-fact as she'd pointed out that she had a business to run and Monday was her busiest day in her office.

At the time, Lisa had felt quite proud of her resolve not to be at Jack's total beck and call. Because she knew she could have made time to meet him on the Monday afternoon. But the moment he drove away, she'd been consumed with instant regret, plus an awful, empty feeling.

It swamped her again, bringing a sigh to her lips.

Her mother threw her a questioning glance over her shoulder. 'You sound like you could do with a strong cup of coffee.'

'I'd love one,' Lisa replied with a grateful smile. She'd refused Jack's offer of brunch this morning, anxious to get home after sleeping in terribly late.

When she pulled out a chair to sit down at her mother's large kitchen table, Lisa's mind suddenly shot back to when she'd sat at Jack's breakfast bar last night, in the nude.

She'd never felt so shamed—yet so excited—in her life.

Her mother turned from where she was making the coffee at the nearby bench. 'By the way, Cory's over at the neighbours' place, if you were wondering. They have their grandkids up for the weekend. One of them's a boy of twelve and very responsible, so you don't have to worry.'

Guilt consumed Lisa when she realised she hadn't been wondering. Or worrying. Cory seemed to have taken a back-seat in her thoughts all of a sudden. Now, that was truly shameful! And not to be tolerated. Her son was the most important person in her life. She would not let a playboy like Jack Cassidy supplant him in either her thoughts, or her heart.

'Has he been a good boy?' she asked, trying desperately to revert to the caring, over-protective mother she usually was.

'He's been a typical boy, Lisa. Boys are rarely good all the time. But who would want that? Nothing worse than a goody-two-shoes boy. They grow up into wimpy, wishy-washy men. By the way, he says he wants to be a soldier when he grows up.'

'A soldier! I thought he wanted to become a doctor!'

'Not since he saw a movie on TV last night about commandos.'

'Mum, you haven't been letting him watch violence, have you?'

Her mother looked sheepish. 'Only the bad guys got killed.'

'You know I don't approve of violence in movies.'

'Well, at least there wasn't any sex,' her mother said defensively. 'I know you don't like him watching sex in movies. But then, neither do you,' she added with that look she always gave Lisa whenever sex was mentioned. As if she was a prude.

If only she knew, Lisa thought, several images flashing into her mind from the night before. The episode in the spa had been pretty incredible, but didn't compare with their raunchy encounter on the terrace, with her gripping the railing and Jack behind her.

Lisa's mouth dried just thinking about how *that* had felt.

'I don't mind a bit of sex in movies,' she said. 'Just not over-the-top stuff.'

You little hypocrite, came that brutally honest voice which kept popping into her head. But…remember that movie where they had sex on the kitchen sink? You haven't tried that yet. Or in the shower. People were always doing it in the shower in movies.

There was no doubt water felt very erotic, when you didn't have any clothes on.

'So what time did you get to bed?' her mother asked as she carried two steaming mugs of coffee over to the table.

'I'm not sure. Two-ish, maybe?' She just hadn't gone to sleep.

'I did try to call you around eleven this morning to ask if it was OK for Cory to go next door, but you didn't answer.'

'I was still sound asleep,' she replied quite truthfully.

'But your phone is right next to your bed.'

'I didn't sleep there. I crashed on the lounge downstairs.'

'Sounds like you had too much to drink.'

'The champagne was free.' And flowing right down her throat at a rate of knots.

'Lucky you. Was your boyfriend there?'

'Who? Oh, you mean Nick Freeman.'

'Yep. Nick Freeman. Did he win an award?'

'Yes. The Golden Gun award. For best thriller of the year. And you were right. That's not his real name. His real name is Jack Cassidy.' Lord, how cool she sounded. Was this what getting tangled up with a wicked man did to you? Made you into an actress as well as a nymphomaniac?

'Jack. Yes, that sounds right. That's a good name for a man of action. Is he good-looking?'

'Tall, dark and handsome. Though on the macho side. He's no pretty boy.'

'Sounds yummy. How old?'

'Mid-to-late thirties.'

'Girlfriend?'

'He came with a blonde.'

'Typical. Hal likes blondes.'

Lisa didn't like being reminded of that. Or how much Jack was like Hal.

Her mother sighed, rather like Jack's fans had last night.

'I'll definitely have to read all those books again one day,' she said. 'But not just yet. They're too fresh in my mind. Did you read any of *The Scales of Justice* yesterday?'

'No. I didn't get the time. But I will. I'd like to read the whole series again, too. Could you get the rest of them for me while I'm here?'

'Sure thing.'

'Are you going to read *all* those books, Mum?' Cory asked on the way home.

'Yes, Cory, I am.'

'But when? You never have time to do anything I want to do.'

Lisa rolled her eyes. Children. They always threw things back at you. 'I read when I go to bed at night, *after* you go to sleep.'

'I hate going to sleep,' Cory grumbled. 'You make me go to bed too early. I don't have to go to bed that early at Grandma's. We watched this beaut movie last night. It was all about… Oops.'

'It's OK, Cory. Mum told me all about it.'

Cory's big blue eyes grew into saucers. 'She *told* you? But she said she'd get into big trouble if you ever found out. Did you go mad on her?'

'Not really, Cory. But you know I don't like you watching violent movies.'

'It wasn't really violent, Mum. It was great. The hero was great. I'm going to be a soldier just like him when I grow up. Jason and I played soldiers today. Can I go back to Grandma's next weekend, Mum? She said I could. Jason's coming up from Sydney again and he wants me to come over and play with him.'

Was fate being kind? Or cruel?

'Please, Mum,' Cory begged.

'If you're a good boy,' she replied, trying to keep her excitement in check. 'And go to bed when I tell you to.'

'I promise, Mum. And I'll clean my teeth without you asking.'

'Now, that would be a first! OK, if you go to bed without whinging and clean your teeth without my telling you, then you can go to Grandma's next weekend.'

'Oh, wow! Wait till I tell Grandma.'

For the first time, Lisa didn't feel jealous over her son's obvious delight at spending more time at his grandma's. She was already thinking how this would leave her totally free to be with Jack again, for the whole weekend, without having to worry about Cory. She could leave her mother's hat off for a while and just be...what, exactly?

A budding nymphomaniac? Or just a girl who'd discovered her sexuality a little late in life and wanted to experience all she'd missed out on?

A third answer jumped into Lisa's mind, one which made her stomach turn over.

Maybe she was simply acting like a female who had finally fallen—not into lust—but in love. Maybe this sexually driven woman she'd become had nothing to do with hormones, but her heart.

Lisa felt sick at the thought she might have fallen in love with Jack. What a total waste of time that would be!

Still, she supposed being in love with the man was more acceptable than being a sex addict.

'Mum,' Cory suddenly piped up, 'you've gone past our street again.'

Lisa groaned. 'Sorry, love.'

'No worries.'

When she pulled into the kerb and waited for the traffic to clear, Cory smiled over at her.

'You look very pretty today, Mum.'

'Do I?' She didn't think so. But everyone was saying it. Jack. Her mother. And now her son.

'Yeah. You look great.'

'Thank you, Cory,' Lisa said, flushing with pleasure.

'When I grow up, I'm going to marry a girl just like you.'

Tears suddenly pricked at Lisa's eyes. It was the nicest thing her son had ever said to her.

'Mum, you're crying!' Cory exclaimed, looking shocked.

'Of course I'm not!' she denied as she dashed the tears away. 'I just had something in my eye.'

Cory looked unconvinced, and remained very quiet during the short drive home.

'I'm going to go upstairs and get ready for my bath,' he offered as soon as they were inside the door.

'What a good idea,' Lisa said with a weary sigh.

All of a sudden she felt very tired. And very fragile.

Hopefully, she would sleep well tonight. And hopefully, in the morning, she would find some much needed strength of character.

CHAPTER FIFTEEN

LISA found she could not go to sleep. Her mind would not relax, along with her body. In the end she sat up in bed, rereading *The Scales of Justice*, and trying to work out just how much of Hal Hunter was Jack in disguise.

Hal's parents were killed tragically, as Jack's had been, but not in a road accident. In a terrorist attack at a foreign holiday resort. Hal grew up obsessed with the idea of justice, but also revenge. He resolved never to feel as powerless as he did on the day his parents were killed, virtually in front of his fourteen-year-old eyes.

That was obviously how Jack had felt when his parents were killed, and when the man responsible didn't get the punishment he deserved. Jack couldn't do much about the situation at the time without breaking the law. But Lisa imagined he gained great satisfaction in giving his fictional male protagonist the ways and means to wreak havoc and revenge on all bad guys.

In the first book, Hal used his inherited fortune to learn everything he needed to know to become a successful one-man vigilante. The teenage Hal was already physically strong and mentally brilliant, but he developed those qualities further with hard work. He increased his wealth with clever investments and cultivated powerful friends, some good, some not so good. Politicians, as well as media magnates and takeover tycoons. He bought an international-news bureau so that he could find out exactly what was going on, anywhere in the world.

And all the while he was searching for the leader of the terrorist group who had claimed responsibility for the killing of his parents and a couple of hundred other innocent people.

Lisa knew from having read the book before that Hal finally found the leader, and killed him. Hal also seduced and then executed a female member of the terrorist gang, *after* finding out an address he needed.

Hal's ruthlessness where women were concerned had permeated the whole series so far, as had his abilities in the bedroom. He would use his sexual skills to find out information, and to exact revenge. He would often sleep with the mistresses and wives of bad guys, not turning a hair when some of these women fell in love with him. He never fell in love himself and never stayed with a woman for long.

Lisa was wondering how long *she* was going to last when the phone beside her bed rang.

For a second she hesitated, worried it might be Jack. She really didn't want to talk to Jack tonight. At the same time, she didn't want the rather loud ring waking Cory up. He was in the bedroom next to hers, after all.

Grimacing, she snatched up the receiver. 'Hello?' Her tone was quite short.

'Hi, Lisa. It's Gail. Sorry to bother you on your home phone on a Sunday night but I thought I should speak to you personally.'

'Oh? What's up? Your ankle not healing well?

'No. It's a lot better. But I still won't be able to clean Jack Cassidy's place next Friday. Or any other Friday, for that matter.'

'Why? What else has happened?'

'Nothing terrible. Phil's got himself a new job. The pay's very good and he said if I didn't want to, I wouldn't have to do cleaning any more. To be honest, Lisa, I hate cleaning. It's enough to do my own place. So I won't be back. I'm sorry. You've been very good to me and I don't like to let you down. But you should be able to find someone else before Friday.'

'Don't worry, Gail,' she said. 'Everything will be fine. And I'm pleased about your husband's job. You deserve a change of luck. If you ever want to come back, just give me a call.'

Gail laughed. 'I won't be doing that. Not unless Phil gets laid off again. Look, I'll probably see you up at the school tomorrow, but I thought I should let you know straight away. I did try and ring you last night, and again this morning, but there wasn't any answer.'

'I was out.' Plus she'd forgotten to put her answering machine on. Ever since Jack had come into her life she'd been in a spin.

'You know, you should marry again, Lisa,' came the unexpected word of advice from Gail.

The wave of dismay which suddenly washed through Lisa made her want to groan.

Because she knew what it meant. She was definitely falling in love with Jack. No use pretending—or hoping—that what she was suffering from was just lust.

Let's face it, Lisa, why else would you be devouring his books again, looking for answers to his complex and unusual persona? And why, most telling of all, would Gail's advice to marry again leave you feeling so suddenly bereft?

Because Jack will never marry you, that's why. All he wants from you is some company at best, along with lots of sex.

How perverse, Lisa thought, that her own discovering the pleasures of the flesh would come with the promise of future misery.

Her own.

'I don't think that'll ever happen, Gail,' she said a bit sharply. 'I'll see you tomorrow. Bye.'

She hung up just in time before tears flooded her eyes. Sighing, she jumped off the bed and hurried into her small *en suite* bathroom, snatching some tissues from the box on the vanity unit and blowing her nose furiously.

The sight of her distressed face in the mirror brought total exasperation with herself.

What's happening to me? I never cry. Now I've done it twice today. All because of that infernal man. I wish I'd never met him. Wish I'd never read his rotten books. I'll bet he's not sitting around his penthouse, blubbering like some baby. Or even giving me a second thought. He's probably sitting at his computer, thinking up more ruthless adventures for his cold-blooded alter ego. *And* giving him more silly women to seduce.

Blondes, of course!

As Lisa marched back to bed and snatched up *The Scales of Justice* once more, Jack was indeed sitting at his computer, attempting to start a new book. He still had one book to deliver on his present contract, a year from today. Which seemed a long time ahead. But Jack knew from experience that if he took too long a break from writing, he found it hard to get back into it.

Yet he hadn't typed a single word after 'CHAPTER ONE'.

Jack had writer's block as he'd never had it before.

'It's all that impossible woman's fault!' he declared, slamming his hands down hard on his desk and levering himself upright.

Why couldn't she be like other women he'd known? he thought irritably as he headed for the bar in the living room. Just when he thought she was putty in his hands, Lisa had pulled back and gone all ice princess on him again.

Jack knew she could have found time for him tomorrow. Even worse was his conviction that she *wanted* to be with him.

But no. The cold light of morning had brought with it a return to the old uptight Lisa. The passionate girl who'd thrilled to his making wild love to her on the terrace in the moonlight had been locked away again, not to be released till she decided it was the right time.

Lisa obviously had an obsession with control. Losing it frightened her.

Yet when she did…

Jack's body leapt at the memory of how she'd lost it last night. Not once, but several times. He loved seeing that glazed look in her eyes, and feeling her body tighten as it did just before she came.

He'd become addicted to making her come. Addicted to how she was with him afterwards, so soft and sweet and utterly his.

He hadn't liked it when she wouldn't go along with what he wanted today.

Not that he'd shown his displeasure. Jack knew that wasn't the way to win a woman like Lisa over. He'd pretended to go along with what she wanted, despite feeling quite desperate to make love to her again. In truth, Jack had found keeping his hands off her this morning a real struggle. Having her in his arms had become more than a need. It was now an obsession, with his increasingly demanding desires in danger of running amok.

From the moment he'd dropped her off at her house, Jack had begun working on a strategy to undermine Lisa's obvious resolve to keep a rein on her own desires.

Which was probably why he couldn't put his mind to thinking up a new plot. The plotting area of his brain was already in use, though not too successfully as yet.

A large Scotch might help, Jack decided as he picked up a fresh bottle of whisky, unscrewed the cap and filled half a glass. To that he added some ice from the bar fridge and carried it down to his home theatre.

Picking up the remote, he settled into the large leather sofa and switched on the TV, flicking through the selection of movies available, choosing a romantic comedy about a pair of mismatched lovers who finally got it together.

'With a bit of luck,' Jack muttered between deep swallows of whisky, 'it might give me some ideas.'

CHAPTER SIXTEEN

LISA sighed, then glanced at the small silver clock she kept on top of her computer. Only eleven.

The morning had seemed endless; she had been constantly tempted by the thought of being with Jack, a much more exciting prospect than doing the same tedious things she always did every Monday morning: take down all the messages on the answering machine and attend to them; update the files and rearrange any of the rosters which had to be rearranged; answer all the emails which had come in through her website; ring any potential clients who had left numbers...

She'd made it sound to Jack as if she'd be flat-out all day. But in truth, she was already on top of everything. She could easily drive out to his place after lunch. Or even before lunch.

He could have *her* for lunch.

Lisa's stomach crunched down hard at the memory of how he'd done that to her by the pool. Spread her out on the tiles and feasted on her till she'd come several times. He seemed to really like doing that to her. And she couldn't get enough of it. She groaned at the thought of him doing that to her right now. Making her forget everything but the pleasure of his tongue sliding over her, and into her...

Lisa shuddered, stunned that she was so turned on just thinking about it.

How easy it would be to ring him and tell him she was on her way over.

Easy, but pathetically weak.

Lisa didn't want Jack to see her as one of those women who came running whenever he snapped his fingers.

Which she could very well become.

Bad enough she was going to his place tomorrow on the pretext of cleaning his study. She knew very well there wouldn't be much cleaning done. And what about Friday? She'd be back there again, on Friday, once again with the excuse of cleaning his place.

Because no way was she going to let some other woman near him. Most of her cleaners were fairly young and some quite attractive. And sex mad, in her opinion.

A bit like you, came that brutally honest voice.

Her front doorbell ringing startled Lisa.

'Oh, lord!' she groaned, jumping up from her desk. 'Please don't let it be Jack.' Not whilst she was hopelessly turned on.

Running from the office, Lisa bolted along the hallway to the upstairs landing, where there was a window overlooking the street below.

The sight of a white van parked outside her house, and not Jack's black Porsche, brought relief and disappointment, Lisa's mixed emotions indicative of her torn frame of mind.

As she made her way more slowly downstairs, she wondered who it could possibly be. A lost tradesman perhaps?

No. Someone selling something more likely.

It was a young woman, holding the most glorious arrangement of red roses.

'Lisa Chapman?' she asked briskly.

'Yes. That's me.'

'Lucky you,' she said with a knowing smile as she handed her the flowers. 'There's a note attached,' she pointed out. 'Have a nice day.'

Lisa stared at the roses as she carried them inside, knowing before she glanced at the note who they were from. Her hands were shaking by the time she placed them in the middle of her dining table and detached the note.

'For a very special lady,' she read. 'Jack.'

Lisa's eyes immediately moistened.

She could not remember the last time she'd received flowers.

'Oh, Jack,' she cried softly as she lifted one of the red roses to her mouth, rubbing the dark, velvety petals back and forth across her lips. 'If only you knew how much I want to just say yes to anything you ask of me.'

Lisa was in danger of succumbing to tears again when her phone rang. She pulled a face, then pulled herself together. Her mother, no doubt. Not a day went by without her mother ringing her at some stage.

Poking the rose back into the arrangement, Lisa

walked back into the family room, where there was an extension on the kitchen bench. Scooping in a gathering breath, she picked up the receiver.

'Hello?'

'Did the flowers come?'

Lisa's heart stopped momentarily before lurching back into a quickened beat.

'Jack,' she said a bit breathlessly.

'The one and only. And the flowers?'

'They...they just arrived.'

'And?'

'They're beautiful.'

'Red roses, I hope. I ordered them over the phone first thing this morning. When I told the florist I wanted two dozen red roses delivered within two hours she said she couldn't promise. But she'd try.'

'They're here and they're exquisite,' Lisa said. 'But horribly expensive, I would imagine. Really, Jack, you shouldn't have.'

'I told you I wanted to spoil you rotten.'

Impossible not to feel ridiculously pleased. And flattered.

'I'll have to hide them, you know. I can't let Cory see them. Or my mother. She drops in sometimes. Unexpectedly.'

'I didn't send you roses for you to hide them, Lisa,' he said with exasperation in his voice. 'Why don't you say they're from a grateful client? It's close to the truth.'

'Two dozen red roses? You think my mother would believe that?'

'Truly, you're a difficult woman. OK, but I refuse to let you hide them. Bring them with you when you come tomorrow and we'll put them to good use.'

'What on earth are you talking about?' Lisa asked, perplexed.

'That's for me to know and you to find out.'

'Might I remind you that I'm supposed to be cleaning your study tomorrow,' she said archly, even whilst her body thrilled to the thought of him doing erotic things to her with the roses.

'And so you shall. You can even wear that adorable apron of yours. The one with the bib and the tie round the back. Though, of course, nothing else. Except perfume and shoes. Yes, high heels would look good. Stilettos, with open toes. And you should paint your toenails and mouth red. A deep red, like the roses.'

Lisa was horrified by the picture he was painting of her.

Horrified, but horribly excited.

'You don't honestly expect me to do all that, do you?'

'Expect? No. But a man can hope…'

'You're a wicked man, Jack Cassidy.'

'Not wicked, Lisa. Infatuated. With you.'

'Oh…'

'You took my breath away at the weekend, do you know that? I can't stop thinking about you. I want you every single minute of the day. I'm going insane with wanting you. I tried to write today but I couldn't. Because my mind is too full of you.'

'Please don't talk to me like this,' she begged, her head whirling with the wild passion in his voice.

'Why not? Why shouldn't I tell you how much I want you?'

'Because…'

'Because you want me the same way, don't you?'

'I…I…'

'I know you find it hard to admit. It's all too new. I could sense that in you yesterday. You wanted to run away from your feelings. You're scared. But you needn't be. I won't hurt you, Lisa. I promise.'

'Promises are just words, Jack. And words come cheap.'

'Not with me,' he ground out. 'My word is my bond. I never go back on my word.'

'Then promise me that you won't try to turn me into some mindless plaything with no will of my own.'

'Is that what you think I'm trying to do?'

'It's what I *know* you're trying to do. Why else would you suggest my cleaning your place in just an apron and stilettos? If you truly like me and respect me, it should be enough that I'm there, with you. You shouldn't need to dress me up like some whore.'

The sudden silence from the other end of the line brought a degree of panic. She'd done it now.

'I…I'm sorry, Jack,' she choked out. 'But that's how it sounded to me.'

'No, no, you're right. I keep forgetting that you're different.'

'Different from what?' she snapped. 'From your usual lay? I suppose you think I'm pretty boring.'

'I think you're very special. And not boring at all. But you are still slightly uptight about sex. Making love can be fun. It doesn't always have to be deadly serious. Dressing up is just a game, Lisa. I'm sorry you took offence at it.'

'No, no. I'm the one who's sorry. You're right. And yes, I am afraid. I'd really like to dress up like that for you, Jack. But I…I just don't have the confidence. Or the courage.'

'You have more courage than any girl I've ever met,' he said with flattering fierceness.

Lisa let out a long, shuddering sigh of surrender. 'You're too strong for me.'

'What do you mean by that?'

'Nothing. Everything. Please let me go now. I…I'll see you tomorrow.'

'What time tomorrow?'

'I'll come as soon as I've dropped Cory off at school.'

'I'm already counting down the hours. Take care, Lisa.'

'And you,' she replied, though a bit stiffly.

He hung up before her, Lisa staring into the dead phone for several seconds.

Slowly, and with a worried frown on her face, she shook her head from side to side. He *was* way too strong for her. Sexually, she was already his, till he decided otherwise. Which he would, one day. Men like Jack didn't stay loyal forever.

All she could do was keep him out of her son's life till that day came.

That part I *can* control, Lisa vowed fiercely.

And I will!

CHAPTER SEVENTEEN

'YOU didn't bring the roses,' was the first thing Jack said when he let her in the following morning.

Lisa swallowed as she gazed up into his eyes. She'd forgotten how good-looking he was. And how big.

He looked even bigger in the loose white trousers and sleeveless black T-shirt he was wearing, clothes which showed off the wearer's tan. And muscles, if he had them.

Jack had them. Oodles of them.

Despite his casual dress and bare feet, he had shaved that morning, she noted. And was wearing cologne, a sandalwood scent which she liked.

'I forgot them,' she replied.

A lie, of course. But how could she possibly put two dozen red roses in the car with her whilst she'd taken Cory to school? He'd have asked her about them. As it was, she'd had to hide them at the back of a high shelf in her walk-in wardrobe before he came home from school yesterday.

Lisa supposed she could have gone back home after dropping Cory off to get them, but she'd wanted to drive straight on here.

She hadn't, however, forgotten the apron. Or the high heels. White, they were. Backless, with open toes. She was wearing them, along with the same white Capri pants and brown singlet top she'd worn last Friday. She was also wearing her sexiest underwear, a cream satin half-cup bra and matching thong which she'd bought at a lingerie sale not long back and never worn.

Lisa had drawn the line at the red nails and lipstick, however, opting instead for a nice bronze colour.

'You've put your hair up again,' Jack said disapprovingly.

'I always put it up when I'm cleaning,' she told him.

His dark brows beetled together in a frustrated frown. 'Come with me.'

He grabbed her hand and pulled her down the hallway to the study door, which was open.

'Oh!' she exclaimed, once she'd looked into the room. 'It's all clean.' Not just clean but also perfectly tidy, with not a scrap of paper on his desk, or a book out of place on the shelves.

'I did it yesterday after our phone call.'

She turned and looked up into his eyes, her own carrying confusion. 'But why, Jack?' She'd spent all night screwing up the courage to clean his study wearing nothing but her apron, thinking that was what he wanted of her.

'Because I decided I didn't want you to spend one second whilst you were with me doing anything other than you making love to me.'

Lisa's relief was short-lived. 'Did you say *me* making love to *you*?'

'Absolutely.'

'But…but I won't know what to do!'

'You're a well-read girl, Lisa. You *do* know what to do.'

So it had come to that already.

Lisa tried to swallow the huge lump which immediately filled her throat, without much success.

'Shall we adjourn to the bedroom?' Jack suggested.

Lisa knew immediately she couldn't do this coldly.

'Would…would you kiss me first, Jack, the way you did the other night?'

Would he kiss her?

Jack suspected, if he started kissing her, he wouldn't be able to stop. He'd thought of nothing else but being with her since Sunday. By the time she'd arrived this morning, he'd resolved not to play time-wasting games. His intention had been to make immediate love to her, then keep her in bed with him most of the day, breaking only for lunch.

Why he'd challenged her to make love to him, he had no idea. That had come right out of left-field. But the idea excited him so much that he refused to back down.

'No,' he said firmly. 'You kiss me.'

She's not ready for this, his conscience castigated him when her already vulnerable blue eyes widened appreciably.

Too late, his male ego countered. The game had begun and he was on the field, making the play and thinking excitedly of the results.

If Jack was brutally honest, he'd wanted to break down all her defences right from the start. More than anything he'd wanted to see this beautiful ice princess lose that iron control which she prized so highly, but which had never brought her any happiness.

For a long moment she just stared up at him, but then the most amazing determination entered her wide-eyed gaze. With measured movements, she lifted her hold-all from her shoulder and walked over to put it on his desk. Then she turned and walked back to where he was still standing in the doorway of his study, her eyes having gone a dark, smoky blue. Once there, she startled Jack by taking his hand and leading him towards the bedroom.

'You're too tall for me to kiss you properly, Jack,' she said on the way. 'You need to be lying down.'

How cool she sounded! How in control!

Exasperation joined his frustration. Wasn't that just so typical of her?

By the time Jack lay down on the bed, his own normally excellent control was already teetering, his flesh under fire as hot blood pumped through him at a rate of knots.

He watched her with a drying mouth as she kicked off her shoes then stretched out beside him on one elbow, leaning over him till her mouth hovered just over his.

'Don't forget this was your idea,' she said, her suddenly trembling voice betraying her underlying nerves.

She kissed him. Very lightly, her lips brushing back and forth across his.

Such a ridiculously sweet kiss, yet it made Jack moan.

Her head shot up to stare down at him with anxious eyes.

'Did I do something wrong?'

'Not that I noticed.'

She smiled a sweet smile, then frowned, as though trying to work out something. 'I…I think I want you naked,' she said at last.

Now it was his turn to stare up at her. 'Naked?'

'Yes, please.'

She was saying please.

Jack scrambled out of his clothes with indecent haste, smothering a sigh of relief at the release of his pained flesh.

'Heavens,' she said when she glanced down at him.

'More like hell,' Jack returned drily. 'Now, how about you?'

She smiled. Not a sweet smile at all this time. A siren's smile.

'All right,' she agreed, climbing off the bed and stunning Jack by starting a slow striptease. Not clumsily, either. Very sexily, lifting her top off first whilst she moved her hips sinuously to some unheard music in her head.

Her cream satin bra was utterly delicious, just covering her nipples. Jack waited with bated breath for her to remove it next, but she didn't. She let her hair down first, finger-combing it sensuously over her shoulders before she finally unhooked her bra and tossed it carelessly aside.

During his days in the army, Jack had seen quite a few stripteases. Some by skilful dancers with incredibly voluptuous bodies. But none had done for him what Lisa's simple striptease was doing. When her hands dropped to her white hipster trousers, his loudly thudding heart literally stopped in his chest. By the time she was standing in front of him wearing cream satin panties which were even more provocative than her bra, Jack's desire had reached the point of no return. How he was going to stand it when she took that last scrap of clothing off, he did not know.

With a mad mixture of pain and pleasure, he soon discovered.

There was nothing ice princess about her now. She'd become one hot babe, half closing her eyes and running her hands over her naked curves in a way which made Jack struggle to stay silent and still on that bed.

Lisa could hardly believe she was doing what she was doing. Yet she thrilled to her own boldness. Thrilled at the way Jack was looking at her. As if she was the sexiest thing on the planet.

Lisa felt more than sexy. She felt wild. And wanton.

By the time she rejoined him on the bed and kissed his mouth once more, her hands had developed a mind of their own. And an independent agenda. They weren't shy at all. Or concerned by their own lack of experience. They seemed to know exactly what to do and where to go.

Maybe Jack was right. Maybe all those sex scenes she'd read in his books had been imprinted on her memory, the well-described techniques waiting to be recalled at this precise moment.

Her left hand cupped the nape of his neck whilst her right hand roved over his body, unerring in its sense of direction, faultless in its instinctive knowledge of just what he would like. It skimmed down his chest towards his stomach, just brushing the tip of his erection before moving over to caress his hip. Very slowly, it travelled down his outer thigh before drifting across between his legs then moving upwards.

His loud groan startled her, her mouth lifting from his.

'Don't stop,' he ground out.

She loved the wild look in his eyes, and the gravelly note in his voice.

She didn't stop, her hand turning over to trail her fingernails lightly over his groin. Her hand reached then encircled the base of his erection. She kissed it, then her lips instinctively parted. Surprisingly, the feel of Jack in her mouth didn't repulse her at all. She thrilled to the unexpected discovery that she *liked* it. Liked making love to him this way.

Because that was what it was. Making love. Giving him pleasure. She could hear his pleasure in the sounds he was making.

Her mouth moved up and down in a slow, sensual rhythm, her hands loving him at the same time. She did not stop when he cried out her name. Or when his hands wound into her hair. She knew he liked this. Hal always did.

I have to stop her, Jack agonised even as his will to do so was disintegrating.

His body was rushing towards a climax. She would hate that, he worried. And so would he.

Because she would think afterwards that he'd turned her into his whore. Yet that was so far from the truth it wasn't funny. She was the woman he loved. He could finally admit it. He loved her. This wasn't just lust. This was far deeper than that.

Lust would let her go all the way. Lust wouldn't care what she felt like afterwards.

His hands were a bit brutal as he yanked her up off him. But there was no time to waste. He rolled her over in a flash and surged into her, groaning as his tortured flesh became enclosed within her deliciously excited body.

He could not possibly last, his body like an active volcano which had been rumbling for far too long. He managed one stroke of his pained flesh inside her. Then two. And then an unexpected three. Maybe, if he concentrated on something else, he could get to five.

Her coming undid him totally, and he just let go, his orgasmic cry both loud and primal, his mind uncaring then of nothing but his own physical release.

Jack did not come back to awareness for quite some time, and when he did Lisa was pushing at his shoulders. More than pushing. She was hitting him.

'Get off me,' she cried. 'Get off!'

Bewildered by her sudden attack on him, Jack stayed right where he was, grabbing her flailing hands and trying to work out why she was reacting like this.

'Stop it, Lisa,' he said, spreading her arms wide and holding her still against the bed.

'But you didn't use anything,' she threw up at him, her face twisted with distress. 'You just went ahead and did it when you knew I wasn't capable of stopping you.'

Aah, so that was the problem. His not using protection.

'It was *me* who couldn't stop, Lisa,' he confessed. 'I was too turned on by what you were doing. I'm sorry. Truly, I am. But I was thinking of you.'

'Thinking of me? How you can say that!'

'I didn't think you'd want me to come in your mouth.'

'Oh, God,' she cried, her eyes squeezing shut as her still flushed face turned away from him.

'I promise you're not in danger of catching anything from me,' he said, upset by her upset. 'You have my word that that is the first time I've ever practised unsafe sex in my life.'

Her expression was pained when she opened her eyes and turned them back to look up at him. 'I could catch a baby.'

Jack withdrew from her abruptly and sat back on his heels, poleaxed. A baby!

'But you said the other night that you were protected from falling pregnant.'

'Not protected, Jack. *Safe*. But only the other night. It wasn't the right time in my cycle for me to conceive. Time has moved on nearly three days since then. I could fall pregnant.'

Jack tried not to panic. Panicking never achieved anything.

'I see,' he said. 'Would a bath help?'

Her look—then her laugh—was quite scathing.

'You don't know as much about a woman's body as you think, do you? No, a bath will not help. What will be, will be.'

Jack grimaced. Damn, but he wished he'd stopped

and put on a condom. But of course, he'd been way past stopping. Way past doing anything but coming.

'I still want to have a shower,' Lisa went on unhappily. 'I feel…yucky.'

Jack sighed as he withdrew. What a disaster!

She looked steadfastly away from his eyes as she scrambled out from under him and half ran to the bathroom, where she slammed the door after her, making him wince.

Jack climbed off the bed himself and pulled on his shorts.

A baby. Good lord.

He was sitting on the side of the bed, still cursing himself, when the bathroom door finally reopened and Lisa came back out, wrapped in a towel and looking very pale.

'So when is your next period actually due?' he asked straight away, trying to assess the risk.

'Sixteen days,' she said precisely. 'I have a twenty-eight-day cycle. Ovulation usually occurs twelve to fourteen days before a period starts.'

'So the odds of your falling pregnant aren't that high.'

'Too high for me,' she said dispiritedly as she started picking up her clothes.

When he tried to help her, she snatched her bra out of his hands and glowered up at him. 'I think you've done enough, don't you?'

'Lisa, don't be like this.'

'Don't be like what?' she snapped. 'You promised you would never hurt me. But you have, in the worst possible way. I don't want to have your baby, Jack. But if a baby does come out of this, then I'll have to.'

'You don't *have* to, Lisa. Not these days.'

'I knew you'd say that,' she threw at him with derision in her face.

'All I meant was that it's your choice, Lisa. It's your body.'

'But it would be *your* baby too, Jack,' she pointed out fiercely. 'I wouldn't be killing just my child. I'd be killing yours.'

Her arguments stunned Jack. Because he'd never looked at abortion like that before.

But she was right. The bottom line was that a life would be taken, a life he'd created. To terminate without any medical reasons for doing so was nothing short of murder.

'I would never ask you to do that, Lisa,' he told her sincerely. 'I've seen too many babies and children heartlessly killed to join that brigade. If you're pregnant, I will stand by you and the baby. I love you, woman, don't you know that?'

Lisa's whole body ceased to function for a few seconds. Her heart and her mind. They just shut down. But a burst of anger jump-started them again.

'Don't you dare say that to me! You don't know what love is, Jack Cassidy. Love would have protected me. Love would not have done what you did today.'

'That's not fair, Lisa. We were both responsible for what happened just now. You could have stopped me, but you didn't. You wanted me as much as I wanted you.'

'That's because you've done what I asked you not

to do. You've turned me into some mindless, sex-mad fool who can't even think straight half the time!' Tears suddenly flooded her eyes. Her head dropped into the clothes she was holding as her shoulders began to shake.

Her inconsolable weeping tore Jack apart. Love sure could make a man feel rotten, he conceded. But it also made him stronger, and more determined.

'Hush,' he said as he came forward and folded her against him. 'You're getting yourself into a right state. And there's no need to. Not yet, anyway. From what you've said, the odds of your falling pregnant are not that high.'

'But what if I am?' she wailed against his chest. 'What will I tell Cory? And my mother? And everyone else?'

'You'll tell them the truth. That you've fallen in love and you're going to have a baby.'

Lisa wrenched out of his arms and glowered up at him. 'I have not fallen in love. You spelt it out for me on Saturday night, Jack. I've fallen in lust, the same as you.'

'I won't argue with you now,' he said, though he didn't look all that pleased.

'I have no intention of arguing with you at all,' she shot back. 'I know what I know, and you won't convince me otherwise. Now I'm going to get dressed. And then I'm going home.'

'Wouldn't it be a better idea if I took you somewhere nice for lunch? Once you calm down, we can talk more rationally.'

'I'm perfectly rational. *Now.* Which is why I'm

going home. *Before* you start doing something to make me go crazy again.'

'All right. If that's what you really want.'

'That's what I really want,' she lied.

'I'll ring you tonight. See how you are.'

'Please don't.'

His eyes blazed like molten steel. 'Don't be ridiculous, Lisa. Call it what you will what's between us, but it's too powerful to ignore. Baby or not, I have to see you again. And if I'm not mistaken, the same applies to you.'

Lisa knew he was right. But be damned if she was going to be so easy in future.

'Cory's going to his grandmother's place again next weekend,' she said stiffly. 'I can see you then.'

'But that's days away!'

'If you love me, like you claim to, you'll be happy to wait.'

'I'm not a waiting kind of man.'

'Love is not selfish,' she argued.

'I just want to *see* you, woman. We don't have to have sex. Look, let me take you to lunch tomorrow. Is that too much to ask?'

'I do my food shopping on a Wednesday,' she said stroppily when she felt herself weakening.

'That's all right. I need to buy food, too. We can shop together, then we can have lunch.'

'All the cold things will melt.'

'In that case, we can have an early lunch, then shop afterwards.'

Lisa sighed. She might as well just say yes and be

done with it. But he wasn't going to get everything his own way.

'All right,' she agreed reluctantly. 'But I'm not going to Erina. I shop at Tuggerah.'

'Tuggerah's fine by me.'

'And I will drive myself in my own car,' she insisted. 'I'll meet you outside the library. At eleven.'

'I'll be there.'

'You have no idea where Tuggerah, or the library, is, do you?'

'I can find them. I'm a big boy.'

Yes, he was just that, she thought irritably. A big boy, wanting what he wants when he wants it. And wheedling and conniving till he gets it. His saying he loved her was just another ploy. Very much like Hal, who told women he loved them all the time to get what he wanted.

'I'm getting dressed now and going home,' she announced for the second time as she scooped up her shoes from the floor.

'I'll make you some coffee before you go,' he offered.

'No!' she snapped. 'No coffee. No food. No nothing!'

Jack stood at the terrace railing, his mind ticking over as he watched her drive off.

She was running for cover again, he realised.

But that was understandable. Everything had happened very quickly between them. Too quickly for a careful girl like Lisa.

Taking risks would worry her. A possible pregnancy would worry her a lot.

Jack had finally got his head around the fact he might have made a baby today. And strangely, now that he'd calmed down himself, he wasn't worried at all. In fact, he rather liked the idea.

Rather amazing for a man who'd thought he never wanted to bring a child into this world.

But that was before he'd met Lisa.

Falling in love with a wonderful girl like her had made him see that *he'd* been running for cover since he left the army.

But he no longer felt consumed with the bitter demons which had plagued him all these years, and which had made him seek a solitary existence, never becoming emotionally involved with anyone or anything.

His emotions were certainly involved now. With this very special and very challenging lady.

His next challenge where Lisa was concerned was to make her see that it wasn't lust binding them together, but love. He also had to make her see that he was husband material.

Oh, yes, he'd changed his mind about marriage as well.

It had been a truly amazing day!

CHAPTER EIGHTEEN

HE WAS already there, outside the library, when she arrived, right on eleven.

Once again, Jack's sophisticated appearance surprised her. He looked very handsome in trendy bone-coloured chinos, a cream and blue striped shirt and smart brown shoes. He was clean-shaven and smelt wonderful.

But it wasn't what he looked like which made her eyes cling to his. It wasn't just lust which swelled in her heart. It was love as well, Lisa had accepted overnight. Because once she'd recovered from the initial shock of possibly conceiving Jack's baby, she found herself secretly thrilled by the idea.

Lust would have been angry at being trapped with a playboy's unwanted child. She didn't feel angry today. She felt weirdly happy.

The depth of her feelings made Lisa extremely nervous, and vulnerable, and needy. She wanted to kiss him. Wanted to hold his hand. Quite desperately.

Instead, she kept her distance and said stiffly, 'You look very smart today.'

'And you look very beautiful,' he returned warmly.

More flattery? Lisa wondered. Or a genuine compliment?

She'd deliberately not gone to too much trouble, dressing in dark blue jeans, a simple white shirt and flat white sandals. She'd left her hair down, curled up slightly on the ends. Her make-up was minimal. The same with her jewellery. Just a gold chain around her neck and gold studs in her ears.

'Come on,' he said. 'Show me to the best eaterie in Tuggerah.'

When he took her hand, Lisa glanced around agitatedly unless someone was watching them. Someone who might know her. But she didn't try to pull her hand away. It felt too good nestled within his large, strong palm.

Still, if she wanted to keep their relationship a secret, she should have chosen a more private and discreet meeting place than a large shopping arcade. All she could do now was minimise the damage, taking him to a café at the other end of the shopping centre which was tucked away in a quiet corner.

Hopefully, no one would see her with Jack there. But to be on the safe side, she put her back to the open side of the café, so that passers-by wouldn't readily notice her.

'Got an email from my editor in London last night,' Jack said after the waitress had taken their order.

'Problems?' Lisa said, happy to discuss anything other than themselves.

'She's having kittens over my last chapter. Says Hal is getting too dark.'

'And is he?'

Jack shrugged. 'Hal's always been dark. So he

seduces a married woman. So what's new? She enjoyed it. And so will the readers.'

Lisa had to admit that they probably would. Hal's wickednesses with women were very exciting to read. Exciting when fiction became reality, too. Regardless of what eventually happened between them, Lisa could never regret her affair with Jack. It had been an incredible experience.

'I'm reading all your books again,' she confessed. 'I started the one set in Africa last night, where all those women and children got massacred and Hal reaps vengeance on their behalf.'

'I reread that one myself sometimes. I like the ending.'

'Did you witness something like that, Jack? For real?'

Jack didn't answer for a few seconds. 'Yeah,' he said, his voice rough. 'Yeah, I did.'

Lisa found his body language very revealing, and reassuring. It was a relief to discover that Jack, unlike Hal, still had a heart. She could see the hurt in his eyes, and hear the pain in his voice.

'How dreadful for you,' she said gently.

His eyes flashed. 'What was even more dreadful was that I couldn't do anything about it. I was ordered not to become involved, yet we were stationed there as a peacekeeping force. Fat lot of peace we kept. That bastard who was running the country at the time was nothing but a homicidal maniac. What I wouldn't have given to be able to shoot him down like the rabid dog he was.'

'So you had Hal torture and murder him instead,' Lisa said.

'Only fictionally. He's still alive somewhere, living off the rewards of his evil.'

'I think you've seen a lot of evil, Jack.'

'*Too* much,' he admitted. 'Not just in Africa, but in other war-torn corners of the world where people do unspeakable things in the name of power and greed. Unfortunately, most of the atrocities committed were against innocent women and children.'

'I can imagine seeing things like that would harden a man.'

Jack shot her a sharp look across the table. 'Let's just say by the time I left the army, I was a candidate for therapy.'

'And did you have therapy?'

Jack laughed. 'Are you kidding? Lying on a psychiatrist's couch isn't my style. Not only that, I'm not sure it would have done any good. Creating Hal became my therapy, just like you so cleverly deduced. He enabled me to give vent to my suppressed need for justice and vengeance. And to release all the hate and anger I had bottled up inside me.'

'I see,' she said, a quiet hope filling her heart. 'And has Hal finished his work yet? Are you feeling better?'

'Much better, actually. I didn't realise how much better till I met you. I'm no longer the emotionally dead man who left the army six years ago, Lisa. I'm no longer Hal, if that's what you're trying to fathom.'

'I suppose I was,' she said, though Lisa suspected there was still a fair bit of Hal left in Jack. Which was perhaps why she'd fallen for him.

Tall, dark and dangerous could be very attractive.

'Look, I understand why you're wary of me, and of letting me into your son's life,' Jack said suddenly. 'And I respect your decision. I can see how important Cory is to you and how protective of him you are. But I want to be more than your secret lover, Lisa. I want our relationship out in the open. Is that too much to ask?'

A great lump had formed in Lisa's throat with his speech. Maybe he did love her a little.

'I guess not,' she said. 'But I still don't want you staying over at my place. Or taking out my son. Or buying him things. Not yet, anyway.'

His face betrayed some annoyance at her demands. 'I'll hang on to that "not yet" bit. But I insist you tell your mother about me. Either that, or let me hire a babysitter occasionally for your son. I want to spend more time with you. I don't want to just snatch an hour or two whilst your boy's at school.'

'Not my mother,' she immediately rejected. 'I'll hire a babysitter myself. *And* pay for her.'

'Aah…Miss Independent.'

'That's the way I am, Jack. I can't help it.'

'It's all right. I like your independence. No one could ever accuse you of wanting me for my money.'

Lisa stared at him. 'Your money?'

'I do have a lot of it, Lisa. If it turns out you're expecting my baby, you can take me for a bundle.'

'How can you ever think I would do such a thing?'

He smiled. 'I don't. But other people might.'

'That's disgusting!'

'Hush up. People are looking over at our table. Which reminds me. When you were talking just then, there was a woman just over there, staring at us like we're visitors from another planet.'

Lisa's head swivelled round.

'No point in looking now,' he said. 'She's gone.'

'What did she look like?'

'Plump. Fiftyish. Attractive in an offbeat way.'

'Please don't tell me she had red hair.'

'Nope. No red hair. She was blonde. Sort of.'

'Thank goodness.'

'Your mum's got red hair?'

'The reddest.'

'Then it was definitely not her. Maybe it was one of your cleaners,' he suggested.

'No. None of them are that old. Could have been someone who thought she recognised you, Jack.'

'Maybe,' he said.

Their food arrived at that moment, two plates of quiche and salad, followed by huge mugs of steaming black coffee.

'It's difficult to keep a secret on the coast,' Lisa muttered after the waitress departed. 'If you go anywhere in public, someone you know is sure to see you.'

'That's why I don't want to keep our relationship a secret. Why not tell your mother and be done with it?'

'Because she thinks you're just it. I wouldn't be able to live with her if she found out about you and me.'

'But you don't live with her, Lisa. You live with your son.'

'She rings me at least once a day.'

'That much.'

'Yes. And drops in all the time. Look, I might tell her, eventually. I might *have* to,' she added, her stomach flipping over at the reminder that she might be pregnant. 'But not yet.'

Jack frowned. 'Is your mother strait-laced, is that it?'

Lisa laughed. 'Oh, no. Mum's had more lovers than you can poke a stick at. I suspect that one of the reasons I grew up frigid was because I didn't want to be like her in any way.'

'I see. Well, you're certainly not frigid any more. Which reminds me. Do you seriously expect me to wait till Saturday before I can see you again? In private, I mean.'

Lisa realised she was being pretty silly, trying to keep him at bay. At the same time, she didn't want him to think her weak.

'I have to come over and clean your place some time this week,' she said.

'No Gail?'

'She's left and I can't find a replacement that quickly.' Lisa tried not to look guilty, but suspected she failed.

'You're lying, Lisa.'

'OK, so I don't want to send you a new cleaner. I'd rather do it myself.'

'You don't trust me.'

'I don't trust other women.'

'You're jealous.'

'Yes, I'm jealous. And possessive. And crazy about you, all right?'

He grinned at her. 'Absolutely all right. So when can I expect you to come and clean? Tomorrow?'

Lisa knew if she raced over to his place tomorrow, nothing would get done for the rest of the week. Sandra always came to do the books on a Thursday and her own house desperately needed cleaning. She'd been very slack lately; too much time spent reading.

'I can't make it till Saturday,' she said.

'Saturday! What about Friday?'

'I do have other things to do, Jack. The business won't run itself.'

'Fair enough. But about Saturday…'

'What about Saturday?'

His eyes locked with hers, his expression passionate and masterful. 'Don't forget to bring that apron with you.'

Lisa had not long arrived home with Cory when her phone started to ring.

'You get on with your homework, Cory,' she instructed him. 'That's sure to be your grandma.'

'Can I talk to her, too?'

'When I've finished.'

He walked off disgruntedly as she picked up the mobile phone. 'Hello,' she said, and headed for the side-door. She would get the washing in and start folding it up whilst her mother chattered away.

'Lisa. It's your mother here.'

Lisa's step faltered. Her mother never called herself *your mother* like that. Not for years, anyway.

'Yes, Mum?'

'I won't beat around the bush. I saw you, Lisa. Today. At Tuggerah. With that man.'

The penny dropped straight away, along with Lisa's stomach. It *had* been her mother staring at them. She must have been to the hairdresser's and changed her hair colour. Again. She did that at least once every two years or so.

'Really? You saw me with my new client? Where?'

'Sitting having coffee in the middle of the mall. A new client, did you say?'

'Yes. He signed up with Clean-in-a-Day not long ago. He's filthy rich and owns a penthouse in Terrigal. Anyway, I ran into him whilst I was shopping and he asked me for coffee.'

'Oh. I thought for a minute there you'd been keeping secrets from me.'

'Mum! Surely you know me better than that.'

'Well, it's not like you to be happy for me to mind Cory two weekends in a row. So when I saw you today with a good-looking man, I thought—'

'You think too much, Mum,' Lisa broke in, then almost laughed. She was sounding just like Jack.

'Actually, he's *very* good-looking, Lisa.'

'I suppose he is.'

'Is he single?'

'Yes, Mum.'

'Did he ask you out?'

'Mum. Don't start.'

'I just want you to be happy.'

'Mum, can we talk about something else? Tell me what you were doing in Tuggerah.'

Thankfully, this launched her mother into a discussion over her change in hair colour. And Jack was forgotten.

But not by Lisa. He was never forgotten. Not for a single moment. He was there, in her head, all the time. Haunting her. Tormenting her.

Today had been very difficult, especially when they went food shopping together. She'd had difficulty keeping her hands off him, wanting to touch him all the time.

Saturday seemed eons away.

CHAPTER NINETEEN

'THIS is absolutely delicious,' Jack said as he put down his fork and picked up his glass of wine. 'You could be a chef, Lisa.'

'I did take a cordon-bleu cooking course,' she admitted, pleased that he liked the stir-fry she'd cooked him. 'I have this compulsion to do everything to the best of my ability. I think it's a hangover from my growing-up years. Like my cleaning fetish. Mum was not the best of housewives. Our house was always a mess. And meals were slapdash affairs. Often little more than snacks. Like baked beans or eggs on toast. Things haven't changed much,' she added with a wry smile. 'That's why Cory likes staying with her so much. Gives him a break from his pain-in-the-neck stickler of a mother.'

'I think his mother is fantastic,' Jack complimented with a sparkle in his eye. 'And I rather like her compulsion to do everything to the best of her ability. Especially in the bedroom.'

Lisa gave him a saucy look. 'I don't recall having been in your bedroom too much today.'

'A mere technicality. You know what I mean.'

Lisa did. Her behaviour from the moment she'd arrived at Jack's penthouse around ten this morning had been exactly as she'd feared. She'd done whatever Jack had demanded of her, starting with cleaning the place in nothing but an apron.

Looking back, however, she felt no shame over the episode. It had been exciting, and fun, Jack following her around and pouncing on her at regular intervals. Not once had they made love in or on his bed. Things had been far more imaginative than that. She had taken her apron off once, to clean his shower, with the water running full bore and Jack in there with her.

By the time the penthouse was thoroughly clean, their insatiable need for each other had been temporarily quelled.

When Jack proposed they go out for a drive, they'd ended up in Erina—a closer shopping centre to Terrigal—where Lisa had bought the ingredients to cook Jack dinner. When they'd returned, they'd made much more leisurely love for a couple of hours. But once again, not in his bed.

When Lisa had confessed to Jack that there'd been a time when she'd been repulsed by watching people make love in movies, he'd been amazed, but understanding.

That was one thing she really liked about Jack. How understanding he was of all her flaws and foibles. It encouraged her to confide in him. To keep nothing secret. She even told him that it *had* been her mother, watching them the other day. With new blonde hair.

'What did you tell your mum you were doing this

weekend?' he suddenly asked, almost as though he'd been reading her mind.

'I said I had a cleaning job today. I explained that Gail had quit without much notice and she had this extremely difficult client with very special requirements who would make a fuss if things weren't done right.'

Jack grinned. 'You're becoming a very inventive girl.'

The highly individual sound of Lisa's mobile phone ringing echoed through the penthouse, making Lisa drop her fork.

'My mobile!' she exclaimed, and jumped up from her chair. It had to be her mother. Lisa had told her to call her on her mobile if there was a problem.

Panic swept in as she raced over to where she'd dropped her hold-all on an armchair. Within seconds, her phone was at her ear.

'Yes, Mum?'

'Lisa…'

Lisa's heart squeezed so tight, she thought she was having a heart attack. In that one word, her mother had conveyed so much. There was a problem. And it was serious.

'What is it?' Lisa demanded to know. 'What's happened to Cory?'

'He…he went to play with Jason next door and he…'

Lisa listened with escalating fear whilst her mother explained that the two boys had been playing commandos in the forest up behind their properties. One would hide and the other had to find him. Just before Cory was due to come home, he hid, and Jason couldn't find him. It seemed he'd gone in too far and become lost. Jason had heard Cory yell out once and then nothing. The police had been called and they did search for a while. But darkness had fallen and they said it was pointless to continue, because there was no moon to help them. Cloud had come in late in the afternoon. The search was due to resume again at daybreak.

'I didn't want to tell you,' her mother said brokenly. 'But I knew you'd be very upset if I didn't. Although there's nothing much you can do tonight.'

'I'll be there as soon as I can,' Lisa said, sounding calm, but feeling anything but.

Jack had by then risen from his chair and was standing near by.

'What is it?' he asked as she clicked off and shoved the phone in her bag.

'It's Cory,' she said, then burst into tears.

Jack took her by the shoulders and shook her. 'Stop that,' he snapped. 'It won't do any good. Just tell me what's happened.'

She told him, gulping down sobs all the while.

'I see,' he bit out, and finally let her go. 'I'll drive. You're not fit. But first, I have to get a few things.'

'What things?' she threw after him as he ran off.

'I'll explain in the car,' he shouted back, and dashed down to his gym room, returning after a couple of minutes with a bag stuffed to the brim with who knew what.

By the time they were underway, Lisa was feeling physically ill. What if they never found Cory? Or if they did, what if he was already dead? What if a snake had bitten him? Or he'd fallen and hit his head? Why else would he not have answered everyone's calls?

'Don't start that catastrophic thinking, Lisa,' Jack advised her in the car. 'I'll find him. Trust me.'

'But how? It's a moonless night. And that bush is terribly thick.'

'Because I was trained in guerrilla warfare. I know how to operate in jungles at night. Plus, I have the right equipment for it. I kept all of it, after I left the army. Just as well I did.'

Jack probably broke the speed limit getting to her mother's place. But Lisa didn't care. The sooner they got there, the better. She also didn't give a damn about her mother finding out about her relationship with him. Nothing was important now but finding her son.

There were no police cars parked in the front yard of her mother's place. Everything looked very quiet. Jack screeched to a halt at the bottom of the front steps, then turned to her.

'I presume we're not going to have any nonsense about your mother knowing who I am, are we?'

'No. No, of course not.'

Her mother came out onto the veranda as Lisa leapt out of the car, her swollen eyes showing the depth of her own distress. Seeing them softened Lisa's underlying anger, for she knew how much her mother loved Cory.

'Oh, Lisa,' her mother cried, a bunch of damp tissues being wrung to death in her hands. 'I'm so sorry. I...I should have made him come home sooner.'

'It's all right, Mum,' she said, sounding a whole lot braver than she felt. 'Jack's going to find Cory for us.'

'Jack?'

Her mother frowned as she stared over Lisa's shoulder at Jack. 'But...I don't understand...'

Jack stepped forward and held out his hand. 'Jack Cassidy, Mrs Chapman. I'm the man you saw having lunch with your daughter the other day. And yes, I'm also Nick Freeman, the writer. But we haven't time for chit-chat at the moment. I need to change clothes quickly, then get you to show me exactly where Cory went into the forest. Here, Lisa, take this mobile phone and put your number into its menu under one. I'll call you as soon as I find Cory.'

'You're going to look for him?' Jill asked. 'Tonight? In the dark?'

'Too right I am,' Jack said as he drew a tracksuit and boots out of his bag. 'Got that mobile number in there yet, Lisa?'

'What? Oh. No. No, I haven't.'

'Then hop to it. Time's a-wasting. Mrs Chapman, could you get me a water bottle and something for Cory to eat, once I've found him? He'll be hungry.'

Both women were happy to be doing something constructive. Lisa even began to feel more hopeful. Jack had an air of competence about him which was very reassuring.

Once changed into his tracksuit and boots, he drew out a torch. 'I have special night glasses to wear later,' he explained. 'Meanwhile, we'll use this.'

Lisa went with them whilst her mother showed Jack where Cory had gone into the bush.

'Can you make it back without the torch?' he asked, and they nodded.

'Good. I might need it. Now, don't you go worrying, my love,' he said to Lisa as he put on the strange-looking night glasses. 'I'll ring you. And I'll find your boy.'

The bush had swallowed him up before Lisa realised she hadn't thanked him.

'Lisa,' her mother said quietly by her side, 'what's been going on between you two?'

Lisa sighed. 'Oh, Mum, please don't ask me that now. All I can think about is Cory at the moment.'

'But…but that's Nick Freeman. *The* Nick Freeman!'

'Oh, all right. I guess this will all be a lot easier if I tell you the truth. Come on, I'll fill you in on the way back to the house.'

Lisa would have liked a camera to record her mother's reaction when she did just that. Jill's expression was priceless. Lisa didn't even bother to water anything down. She told her everything. Even the fact that she'd fallen madly in love with the man. The only bit she left out was that she could possibly be pregnant. She couldn't even think about having another baby when her first precious baby, her darling Cory, was lost out there somewhere.

'I don't believe it,' were the first actual words Jill spoke.

By then they were back at the house, in the kitchen.

'Does *he* love *you*?' she asked.

'He say he does.'

'But you don't believe him.'

'I just don't know, Mum. He's Hal Hunter in disguise, and he wanted to sleep with me.'

'I see. Yes, I see. But Hal's not a bad man, Lisa. Underneath his hard outer shell, he's a hero. That's why his readers love him, and care about him. It's obvious all he needs is to meet the right girl. Which I have no doubt he just has. You are a very special girl, Lisa. How could any man help but fall in love with you?'

'Oh, Mum,' Lisa cried. 'What a lovely thing to say.'

Her mother smiled. 'Here. Give your old mum a hug.'

Lisa was enfolded against her mother's soft bosom when her mobile phone rang. Her heart leapt as she grabbed it off the kitchen table.

'Haven't found him yet, Lisa,' Jack said straight away. 'Thought I'd better check in and see how you're doing.'

'Holding on, Jack. I do feel better knowing you're out there, looking for him.'

'Couldn't let the woman I love worry herself sick all night now, could I?'

Lisa's heart turned over. Not a bad man, her mother had said. A hero.

He was that to her at this moment. And more.

'Oh, Jack, I love you too,' she said, then burst into tears again.

'Did I hear right? Did you just say you love me?'

'Yes,' she sobbed.

'Right. Get off this phone, then, woman. I have a job to do here. I have to find our boy.'

Lisa clicked off and just stared at her mother, tears running down her face.

'I think he does love me, Mum,' Lisa choked out. 'He said he had to find our boy. *Our* boy.'

'Oh Lisa. That's wonderful.'

More than wonderful forty minutes later when her phone rang again.

'I've found him, Lisa. He's all right. Just a badly sprained ankle and a big egg on his head. Tripped over a fallen tree trunk and knocked himself unconscious for a while. I'll have to carry him out, so I'd better stay put for the night. It's a bit hazardous in the dark. He wants to talk to you, but he's worried he's going to get into trouble. I told him no way, but he needs to hear that for himself.'

'Mum?'

Emotion grabbed at her heart and throat, almost choking off her voice.

'Cory,' was all she could manage in a strangled tone.

'I'm all right, Mum. Honest. But there's a rip in my shirt.'

'I don't care about your shirt, darling. As long as you're all right.'

'Yeah. I'm fine. Jack's looking after me.'

Lisa had to smile. So it was Jack, already.

'He said he's your new boyfriend.'

'That's right, Cory.'

'Cool! Did you know he used to be a soldier?'

'Yes, Cory.'

'Mum…'

'Yes, Cory.'

'I love you, Mum.'

Tears welled up in her eyes. 'I love you too, Cory. Could I speak to Jack again, please?'

'Sure.'

'Me here,' he said.

'Thank you,' she choked out.

'You don't have to thank me, Lisa.'

'Yes, I do. Not just for finding Cory, but for really loving me.'

'It wasn't very hard. Which reminds me. Would you reconsider your thoughts on our relationship? One where the girl wears a ring? Or two?'

'Jack! Do you honestly mean that?'

'You'd better believe it. So what's your answer?'

Lisa thought of how she'd only known him for nine days. But it felt like a lifetime. Maybe because she had got to know him so well through his books.

'He wants to marry me,' she whispered to her mother across the table. 'What do you think I should do?'

Jill looked startled. 'You're asking me for *my* advice?'

'Yes, Mum.'

'Go with your heart, daughter. Always go with your heart.'

'Jack?'

'Yes?'

'Yes,' she said. 'Yes, I'd like that very much.'

'Fantastic! We'll go ring-shopping tomorrow. And then I'll take you and Cory out somewhere for a celebration dinner. Is that OK with you?'

'Can I bring Mum as well?'

'Absolutely.'

Lisa sighed, then smiled. Now she knew what it was like to be happy. Really, really happy.

'Take care, Jack,' she said softly.

'I'll see you in the morning,' he returned, his voice all smiles as well. 'Have the coffee ready.'

CHAPTER TWENTY

THE Academy Awards, sixteen months later...

'Grandma! Helene! Mum and Jack are on the telly. They've just got out of the limo. Hurry!'

Helene ran into the hotel suite sitting room first, followed by Jill, who was carrying her five-month-old granddaughter in her arms.

'There they are!' Cory pointed out excitedly.

'Don't they both look absolutely stunning!' Helene exclaimed.

'Like movie stars,' Jill agreed.

Jack took Lisa's elbow as they walked down the red carpet, cameras flashing in their faces all the time. He felt supremely proud of the woman by his side. Dressed in a long, floaty lavender gown, his beautiful wife outshone everyone else, in his opinion.

'Jack! Over here!' an interviewer called out.

When Jack saw the man was from Australia, he guided Lisa towards his microphone.

'How do you feel about *The Scales of Justice* being

nominated for so many awards, Jack?' came the inevi-
table question he'd been asked all week.

'Very surprised,' Jack replied. 'Action thrillers don't
usually rate so highly with the Academy.'

'Aah, but your story is not just a thriller, Jack. It's a
character study.'

'That's very perceptive of you,' Jack complimented.
'Not everyone sees that.'

'I've heard rumours that you won't be writing any
more Hal Hunter stories, is that right?'

'Yep. The last one has just gone to the publisher and
will be out for the American summer.'

'Everyone wants to know if you killed Hal off.'

Jack grinned. 'Sorry. That's a trade secret.'

'Mrs Cassidy! Can you give us any clues?'

Lisa smiled up at Jack. 'Let me just say that you're
in for a surprise.'

'Doesn't sound like he gets killed off, everyone,' the
man announced into the microphone. 'Which will be a
relief to all the Hal Hunter fans out there. Before you
go, Jack, can you tell us what the new book is called?'

'*Retribution and Redemption*. And that's all we're
going to tell you.'

'Your female fans aren't going to like Hal getting
married, Jack,' Lisa whispered to him as they walked
on.

'I don't think they'll mind.'

'But to a cleaner?'

'A beautiful blonde cleaner,' Jack pointed out. 'Who
had his secret love-child two years before.'

'It reads more like a romance than a thriller.'

'But it *is* a romance, my darling. With a happy ending. Just like us.'

Her smile, when she glanced up at him, was why Jack had no need to write Hal Hunter books any more. His life had different needs now. And different goals.

'Have I told you that you look incredibly beautiful tonight?' he said.

'Only about twenty times so far. Do you think we might win tonight, Jack?'

'Never in a million years.'

The Scales of Justice took out every award it was nominated for, including best movie, best director and best screenplay.

Jack and Lisa didn't go to any of the glamorous after-awards parties. They went straight back to the hotel, where Jack's first action was to go in and look at his sleeping daughter.

Lisa hadn't fallen pregnant that first time. So they'd waited till they married before taking any more chances.

Jack had been besotted with his daughter even before she was born. He'd almost cried at Lisa's ultrasound when he saw life moving inside her. The day Jessica had been born, he *had* cried.

'She's like you,' he told his wife when she joined him by the cot.

'With that chin? She's a female image of you, Jack. And just as stubborn.'

'She's an angel,' Jack murmured.

Lisa laughed. 'And I thought you were going to be a firm father.'

'I will be,' he said, taking his wife into his arms, 'once Jess starts dating. I certainly won't let her go out with anyone like me.'

'There are worse things that can happen to a girl,' Lisa murmured, her eyes going all smoky.

Jack kissed her. Then he kissed her again.

Nine months later, Cory had a little brother to go with his little sister. They named him Hal.

REQUEST YOUR FREE BOOKS!

HARLEQUIN® *Presents*

PASSION
GUARANTEED
SEDUCTION

2 FREE NOVELS
PLUS 2
FREE GIFTS!

YES! Please send me 2 FREE Harlequin Presents® novels and my 2 FREE gifts. After receiving them, if I don't wish to receive any more books, I can return the shipping statement marked "cancel." If I don't cancel, I will receive 6 brand-new novels every month and be billed just $3.80 per book in the U.S., or $4.47 per book in Canada, plus 25¢ shipping and handling per book and applicable taxes, if any*. That's a savings of close to 15% off the cover price! I understand that accepting the 2 free books and gifts places me under no obligation to buy anything. I can always return a shipment and cancel at any time. Even if I never buy another book from Harlequin, the two free books and gifts are mine to keep forever.

106 HDN EEXK   306 HDN EEXV

Name _____ (PLEASE PRINT)

Address _____ Apt. #

City _____ State/Prov. _____ Zip/Postal Code

Signature (if under 18, a parent or guardian must sign)

Mail to the Harlequin Reader Service®:

IN U.S.A.
P.O. Box 1867
Buffalo, NY
14240-1867

IN CANADA
P.O. Box 609
Fort Erie, Ontario
L2A 5X3

Not valid to current Harlequin Presents subscribers.

Want to try two free books from another line?
Call 1-800-873-8635 or visit www.morefreebooks.com.

* Terms and prices subject to change without notice. NY residents add applicable sales tax. Canadian residents will be charged applicable provincial taxes and GST. This offer is limited to one order per household. All orders subject to approval. Credit or debit balances in a customer's account(s) may be offset by any other outstanding balance owed by or to the customer. Please allow 4 to 6 weeks for delivery.

HP06

HARLEQUIN *Presents*

POSH DOCS

Dedicated, daring and devastatingly
handsome—these doctors are guaranteed
to raise your temperature!

The new collection by your favorite authors,
available in January 2007:

HER BABY SECRET by Kim Lawrence
THE GREEK CHILDREN'S DOCTOR by Sarah Morgan
HER HONORABLE PLAYBOY by Kate Hardy
SHEIKH SURGEON by Meredith Webber